AUNT JUDY'S
TALES

Mrs Alfred Gatty

1st WORLD
LIBRARY
Literary Society

Aunt Judy's Tales

Mrs. Alfred Gatty

© 1st World Library – Literary Society, 2004
PO Box 2211
Fairfield, IA 52556
www.1stworldlibrary.org
First Edition

LCCN: 2004091263

Softcover ISBN: 1-59540-681-6
eBook ISBN: 1-59540-781-2

Purchase *"Aunt Judy's Tales"*
as a traditional bound book at:
www.1stWorldLibrary.org/purchase.asp?ISBN=1-59540-681-6

1st World Library Literary Society is a nonprofit
organization dedicated to promoting literacy by:

- Creating a free internet library accessible from any
  computer worldwide.
- Hosting writing competitions and offering book
  publishing scholarships.

Readers interested in supporting literacy
through sponsorship, donations or
membership please contact:
literacy@1stworldlibrary.org
Check us out at: www.1stworldlibrary.org

Aunt Judy's Tales
contributed by the Mahaney Family
in support of
1st World Library Literary Society

*TO THE "LITTLE ONES"
IN MANY HOMES,
THIS VOLUME IS DEDICATED.*

M. G.

CONTENTS

The Little Victims. 7

Vegetables out of Place 30

Cook Stories 52

Rabbits' Tails. 80

Out of the Way. 105

Nothing to do. 141

THE LITTLE VICTIMS.

"Save our blessings, Master, save,
From the blight of thankless eye."

Lyra Innocentium.

There is not a more charming sight in the domestic world, than that of an elder girl in a large family, amusing what are called the *little ones.*

How could mamma have ventured upon that cosy nap in the arm-chair by the fire, if she had been harassed by wondering what the children were about? Whereas, as it was, she had overheard No. 8 begging the one they all called "Aunt Judy," to come and tell them a story, and she had beheld Aunt Judy's nod of consent; whereupon she had shut her eyes, and composed herself to sleep quite complacently, under the pleasant conviction that all things were sure to be in a state of peace and security, so long as the children were listening to one of those curious stories of Aunt Judy's, in which, with so much drollery and amusement, there was sure to be mixed up some odd scraps of information, or bits of good advice.

So, mamma being asleep on one side of the fire, and papa reading the newspaper on the other, Aunt Judy and No. 8 noiselessly left the room, and repaired to the large red-curtained dining-room, where the former sat down to concoct her story, while the latter ran off to collect the little ones together.

In less than five minutes' time there was a stream of noise along the passage - a bursting open of the door, and a crowding round the fire, by which Aunt Judy sat.

The "little ones" had arrived in full force and high expectation. We will not venture to state their number. An order from Aunt Judy, that they should take their seats quietly, was but imperfectly obeyed; and a certain amount of hustling and grumbling ensued, which betrayed a rather quarrelsome tendency.

At last, however, the large circle was formed, and the bright firelight danced over sunny curls and eager faces. Aunt Judy glanced her eye round the group; but whatever her opinion as an artist might have been of its general beauty, she was by no means satisfied with the result of her inspection.

"No. 6 and No. 7," cried she, "you are not fit to listen to a story at present. You have come with dirty hands."

No. 6 frowned, and No. 7 broke out at once into a howl; he had washed his hands ever so short a time ago, and had done nothing since but play at knuckle-bones on the floor! Surely people needn't wash their hands every ten minutes! It was very hard!

Aunt Judy had rather a logical turn of mind, so she set about expounding to the "little ones" in general, and to Nos. 6 and 7 in particular, that the proper time for washing people's hands was when their hands were

Mrs Alfred Gatty

dirty; no matter how lately the operation had been performed before. Such, at least, she said, was the custom in England, and everyone ought to be proud of belonging to so clean and respectable a country. She, therefore, insisted that Nos. 6 and 7 should retire up-stairs and perform the necessary ablution, or otherwise they would be turned out, and not allowed to listen to the story.

Nos. 6 and 7 were rather restive. The truth was, it had been one of those unlucky days which now and then will occur in families, in which everything seemed to be perverse and go askew. It was a dark, cold, rainy day in November, and going out had been impossible. The elder boys had worried, and the younger ones had cried. It was Saturday too, and the maids were scouring in all directions, waking every echo in the back-premises by the grating of sand-stone on the flags; and they had been a good deal discomposed by the family effort to play at "Wolf" in the passages. Mamma had been at accounts all the morning, trying to find out some magical corner in which expenses could be reduced between then and the arrival of Christmas bills; and, moreover, it was a half-holiday, and the children had, as they call it, nothing to do.

So Nos. 6 and 7, who had been vexed about several other little matters before, during the course of the day, broke out now on the subject of the washing of their hands.

Aunt Judy was inexorable however - inexorable though cool; and the rest got impatient at the delay which the debate occasioned: so, partly by coaxing, and partly by the threat of being shut out from hearing the story, Nos. 6 and 7 were at last prevailed upon to go up-stairs and wash their grim little paws into that delicate shell-like pink, which is the characteristic of juvenile fingers when clean.

As they went out, however, they murmured, in whimpered tones, that they were sure it was *very hard*!

After their departure, Aunt Judy requested the rest not to talk, and a complete silence ensued, during which one or two of the youngest evidently concluded that she was composing her story, for they stared at her with all their might, as if to discover how she did it.

Meantime the rain beat violently against the panes, and the red curtains swayed to and fro from the effect of the wind, which, in spite of tolerable woodwork, found its way through the divisions of the windows. There was something very dreary in the sound, and very odd in the varying shades of red which appeared upon the curtains as they swerved backwards and forwards in the firelight.

Several of the children observed it, but no one spoke until the footsteps of Nos. 6 and 7 were heard approaching the door, on which a little girl ventured to whisper, "I'm very glad I'm not out in the wind and rain;" and a boy made answer, "Why, who would be so silly as to think of going out in the wind and rain? Nobody, of course!"

At that moment Nos. 6 and 7 entered, and took their places on two little Derby chairs, having previously showed their pink hands in sombre silence to Aunt Judy, whereupon Aunt Judy turned herself so as to face the whole group, and then began her story as follows:-

"There were once upon a time eight little Victims, who were shut up in a large stone-building, where they were watched night and day by a set of huge grown-up keepers, who made them do whatever they chose."

"Don't make it *too* sad, Aunt Judy," murmured No. 8, half in a tremble already.

"You needn't be frightened, No. 8," was the answer; "my stories always end well."

"I'm so glad," chuckled No. 8 with a grin, as he clapped one little fat hand down upon the other on his lap in complete satisfaction. "Go on, please."

"Was the large stone-building a prison, Aunt Judy?" inquired No. 7.

"That depends upon your ideas of a prison," answered Aunt Judy. "What do you suppose a prison is?"

"Oh, a great big place with walls all round, where people are locked up, and can't go in and out as they choose."

"Very well. Then I think you may be allowed to call the place in which the little Victims were kept a prison, for it certainly was a great big place with walls all round, and they were locked up at night, and not allowed to go in and out as they chose."

"Poor things," murmured No. 8; but he consoled himself by recollecting that the story was to end well.

"Aunt Judy, before you go on, do tell us what *victims* are? Are they fairies, or what? I don't know."

This was the request of No. 5, who was rather more thoughtful than the rest, and was apt now and then to delay a story by his inquiring turn of mind.

No. 6 was in a hurry to hear some more, and nudged No. 5 to make him be quiet; but Aunt Judy interposed; said she did not like to tell stories to people who didn't care to know what they meant, and declared that No. 5 was quite right in asking what a victim was.

"A victim," said she, "was the creature which the old heathens used to offer up as a sacrifice, after they had gained a victory in battle. You all remember I dare say," continued she, "what a sacrifice is, and have heard about Abel's sacrifice of the firstlings of his flock."

The children nodded assent, and Aunt Judy went on:-

"No such sacrifices are ever offered up now by us Christians, and so there are no more real *victims* now. But we still use the word, and call any creature a victim who is ill-used, or hurt, or destroyed by some-body else.

"If you, any of you, were to worry or kill the cat, for instance, then the cat would be called *the victim of your cruelty;* and in the same manner the eight little Victims I am going to tell you about were the victims of the whims and cruel prejudices of those who had the charge of them.

"And now, before I proceed any further, I am going to establish a rule, that whenever I tell you anything very sad about the little Victims, you shall all of you groan aloud together. So groan here, if you please, now that you quite understand what a victim is."

Aunt Judy glanced round the circle, and they all groaned together to order, led off by Nos. 3 and 4, who did not, it must be owned, look in a very mournful state while they performed the ceremony.

It was wonderful what good that groan did them all! It seemed to clear off half the troubles of the day, and at its conclusion a smile was visible on every face.

Aunt Judy then proceeded:-

"I do not want to make you cry too much, but I will tell you of the miseries the captive victims underwent in the course of one single day, and then you will be able to judge for yourselves what a life they led together.

"One of their heaviest miseries happened every evening. It was the misery of *going to bed.* Perhaps now you may think it sounds odd that going to bed should be called a misery. But you shall hear how it was.

"In the evening, when all the doors were safely locked and bolted, so that no one could get away, the little Victims were summoned down-stairs, and brought into a room where some of the keepers were sure to be sitting in the greatest luxury. There was generally a warm fire on the hearth, and a beautiful lamp on the table, which shed an agreeable light around, and made everything look so pretty and gay, the hearts of the poor innocent Victims always rose at the sight.

"Sometimes there would be a huge visitor or two present, who would now and then take the Victims on their knees, and say all manner of entertaining things to them. Or there would be nice games for them to play at. Or the keepers themselves would kiss them, and call them kind names, as if they really loved them. How nice all this sounds, does it not? And it would have been nice, if the keepers would but have let it last for ever. But that was just the one thing they never would do, and the consequence was, that, whatever pleasure they might have had, the wretched Victims always ended by being dissatisfied and sad.

"And how could it be otherwise? Just when they were at the height of enjoyment, just when everything was most delightful, a horrible knock was sure to be heard at the door, the meaning of which they all knew but too well. It was the knock which summoned them to bed; and at such a moment you cannot wonder that going to bed was felt to be a misfortune.

"Had there been a single one among them who was sleepy, or tired, or ready for bed, there would have been some excuse for the keepers; but as it was, there was none, for the little Victims never knew what it was to feel tired or weary on those occasions, and were always carried forcibly away before that feeling came on.

"Of course, when the knock was heard, they would begin to cry, and say that it was very hard, and that they didn't *want* to go to bed, and one went so far once as to add that she *wouldn't* go to bed.

"But it was all in vain. The little Victims might as well have attempted to melt a stone wall as those hard-hearted beings who had the charge of them.

Mrs Alfred Gatty

"And now, my dears," observed Aunt Judy, stopping in her account, "this is of all others the exact moment at which you ought to show your sympathy with the sufferers, and groan."

The little ones groaned accordingly, but in a very feeble manner.

Aunt Judy shook her head.

"That groan is not half hearty enough for such a misery. Don't you think, if you tried hard, you could groan a little louder?"

They did try, and succeeded a little better, but cast furtive glances at each other immediately after.

"Were the beds very uncomfortable ones, Aunt Judy?" inquired No. 8, in a subdued voice.

"You shall judge for yourself," was the answer. "They were raised off the floor upon legs, so that no wind from under the door could get at them; and on the flat bottom called the bed-stock, there was placed a thick strong bag called a mattress, which was stuffed with some soft material which made it springy and pleasant to touch or lie down upon. The shape of it was a long square, or what may be called a rectangular parallelogram. I strongly advise you all to learn that word, for it is rather an amusing idea as one steps into bed, to think that one is going to sleep upon a parallelogram."

Nos. 3 and 4 were here unable to contain themselves, but broke into a peal of laughter. The little ones stared.

"Well," resumed Aunt Judy, "for my part, I think it's a very nice thing to learn the ins and outs of one's own life; to consider how one's bed is made, and the why and wherefore of its shape and position. It is a great pity to get so accustomed to things as not to know their value till we lose them! But to proceed.

"On the top of this parallelogramatic mattress was laid a soft blanket. On the top of that blanket, two white sheets. On the top of the sheets, two or more warm blankets, and on the top of the blankets, a spotted cover called a counterpane.

"Now it was between the sheets that each little Victim was laid, and such were the receptacles to which they were unwillingly consigned, night after night of their lives!

"But I have not yet told you half the troubles of this dreadful 'going to bed.' A good fire with a large tub before it, and towels hung over the fender, was always the first sight which met the tearful eyes of the little Victims as they entered the nursery after being torn from the joys of the room down-stairs. And then, lo and behold! a new misery began, for, whether owing to the fatigue of getting up-stairs, or that their feelings had been so much hurt, they generally discovered at this moment that they were one and all so excessively tired, they didn't know what to do; - of all things, did not choose to be washed - and insisted, each of them, on being put to bed first! But let them say what they would, and cry afresh as they pleased, and even snap and snarl at each other like so many small terriers, those cruel keepers of theirs never would grant their requests; never would put any of them to bed dirty, and always declared that it was impossible to put each of

Mrs Alfred Gatty

them to bed first!

Imagine now the feelings of those who had to wait round the fire while the others were attended to! Imagine the weariness, the disgust, before the whole party was finished, and put by for the night!"

Aunt Judy paused, but no one spoke.

"What!" cried she suddenly, "will nobody groan? Then I must groan myself!" which she did, and a most unearthly noise she made; so much so, that two or three of the little ones turned round to look at the swelling red curtains, just to make sure the howl did not proceed from thence.

After which Aunt Judy continued her tale:-

"So much for night and going to bed, about which there is nothing more to relate, as the little Victims were uncommonly good sleepers, and seldom awoke till long after daylight.

"Well now, what do you think? By the time they had had a good night, they felt so comfortable in their beds, that they were quite contented to remain there; and then, of course, their tormentors never rested till they had forced them to get up! Poor little things! Just think of their being made to go to bed at night, when they most disliked it, and then made to get up in the morning, when they wanted to stay in bed! It certainly was, as they always said, 'very, very hard.' This was, of course, a winter misery, when the air was so frosty and cold that it was very unpleasant to jump out into it from a warm nest. Terrible scenes took place on these occasions, I assure you, for sometimes the wretched

Victims would sit shivering on the floor, crying over their socks and shoes instead of putting them on, (which they had no spirit for,) and then the savage creatures who managed them would insult them by irritating speeches.

"'Come, Miss So-and-So,' one would say, 'don't sit fretting there; there's a warm fire, and a nice basin of bread-and-milk waiting for you, if you will only be quick and get ready.'

"Get ready! a nice order indeed! It meant that they must wash themselves and be dressed before they would be allowed to touch a morsel of food.

"But it is of no use dwelling on the unfeelingness of those keepers. One day one of them actually said:-

"'If you knew what it was to have to get up without a fire to come to, and without a breakfast to eat, you would leave off grumbling at nothing.'

"*Nothing*! they called it *nothing* to have to get out of a warm bed into the fresh morning air, and dress before breakfast!

"Well, my dears," pursued Aunt Judy, after waiting here a few seconds, to see if anybody would groan, "I shall take it for granted you feel for the *getting-up* misery as well as the *going-to-bed* one, although you have not groaned as I expected. I will just add, in conclusion, that the summer *getting-up* misery was just the reverse of this winter one. Then the poor little wretches were expected to wait till their nursery was dusted and swept; so there they had to lie, sometimes for half-an-hour, with the sun shining in upon them, not allowed to get up and come out into the dirt and dust!

"Of course, on those occasions they had nothing to do but squabble among themselves and teaze; and I assure you they had every now and then a very pleasant little revenge on their keepers, for they half worried them out of their lives by disturbances and complaints, and at any rate that was some comfort to them, although very often it hindered the nursery from being done half as soon as it would have been if they had been quiet.

"I shall not have time to tell of everything," continued Aunt Judy, "so I must hurry over the breakfast, although the keepers contrived to make even that miserable, by doing all they could to prevent the little Victims from spilling their food on the table and floor, and also by insisting on the poor little things sitting tolerably upright on their seats - *not* lolling with both elbows on the table-cloth - *not* making a mess - not, in short, playing any of those innocent little pranks in which young creatures take delight.

"It was a pitiable spectacle, as you may suppose, to see reasonable beings constrained against their inclinations to sit quietly while they ate their hearty morning meal, which really, perhaps, they might have enjoyed, had they been allowed to amuse themselves in their own fashion at the same time.

"But I must go on now to that great misery of the day, which I shall call the *lesson* misery.

"Now you must know, the little Victims were all born, as young kids, lambs, kittens, and puppy-dogs are, with a decided liking for jumping about and playing all day long. Think, therefore, what their sufferings were when they were placed in chairs round a table, and obliged to sit and stare at queer looking characters in books until they had learned to know them what was called *by heart*. It was a very odd way of describing it, for I am sure they had often no heart in the matter, unless it was a hearty dislike.

"'Tommy Brown in the village never learns any lessons,' cried one of them once to the creature who was teaching him, 'why should I? He is always playing at oyster-dishes in the gutter when I see him, and enjoying himself. I wish *I* might enjoy myself!'

"Poor Victim! He little thought what a tiresome lecture this clever remark of his would bring on his devoted head!

"Don't ask me to repeat it. It amounted merely to this, that twenty years hence he would he very glad he had learnt something else besides making oyster-dishes in the streets. As if that signified to him now! As if it took away the nuisance of having to learn at the present moment, to be told it would be of use hereafter! What was the use of its being of use by-and-by?

"So thought the little Victim, young as he was; so, said he, in a muttering voice:-

"'I don't care about twenty years hence; I want to be happy now!'

"This was unanswerable, as you may suppose; so the puzzled teacher didn't attempt to make a reply, but said:-

Mrs Alfred Gatty

"'Go on with your lessons, you foolish little boy!'

"See what it is to be obstinate," pursued Aunt Judy. "See how it blinds people's eyes, and prevents them from knowing right from wrong! Pray take warning, and never be obstinate yourselves; and meantime, let us have a good hearty groan for the *lesson* misery."

The little ones obeyed, and breathed out a groan that seemed to come from the very depths of their hearts; but somehow or other, as the story proceeded, the faces looked rather less amused, and rather more anxious, than at first.

What could the little ones be thinking about to make them grave?

It was evidently quite a relief when Aunt Judy went on:-

"You will be very much surprised, I dare say," said she, "to hear of the next misery I am going to tell you about. It may be called the *dinner* misery, and the little Victims underwent it every day."

"Did they give them nasty things to eat, Aunt Judy?" murmured No. 8, very anxiously.

"More likely not half enough," suggested No. 5.

"But you promised not to make the story *too* sad, remember!" observed No. 6.

"I did," replied Aunt Judy, "and the *dinner* misery did not consist in nasty food, or there not being enough. They had plenty to eat, I assure you, and everything was good. But - "

Aunt Judy stopped short, and glanced at each of the little ones in succession.

"Make haste, Aunt Judy!" cried No. 8. "But what?"

"*But*," resumed Aunt Judy, in her most impressive tone, "they had to wait between the courses."

Again Aunt Judy paused, and there was a looking hither and thither among the little ones, and a shuffling about on the small Derby chairs, while one or two pairs of eyes were suddenly turned to the fire, as if watching it relieved a certain degree of embarrassment which their owners began to experience.

"It is not every little boy or girl," was Aunt Judy's next remark, "who knows what the courses of a dinner are."

"*I* don't," interposed No. 8, in a distressed voice, as if he had been deeply injured.

"Oh, you think not? Well, not by name, perhaps," answered Aunt Judy. "But I will explain. The courses of a dinner are the different sorts of food, which follow each other one after the other, till dinner is what people call 'over.' Thus, supposing a dinner was to begin with pea-soup, as you have sometimes seen it do, you would expect when it was taken away to see some meat put upon the table, should you not?"

The little ones nodded assent.

"And after the meat was gone, you would expect pie or pudding, eh?"

Mrs Alfred Gatty

They nodded assent again, and with a smile.

"And if after the pudding was carried away, you saw some cheese and celery arrive, it would not startle you very much, would it?"

The little ones did nothing but laugh.

"Very well," pursued Aunt Judy, "such a dinner as we have been talking about consists of four courses. The soup course, the meat course, the pudding course, and the cheese course. And it was while one course was being carried out, and another fetched in, that the little Victims had to wait; and that was the *dinner* misery I spoke about, and a very grievous affair it was. Sometimes they had actually to wait several minutes, with nothing to do but to fidget on their chairs, lean backwards till they toppled over, or forward till some accident occurred at the table. And then, poor little things, if they ventured to get out their knuckle-bones for a game, or took to a little boxing amusement among themselves, or to throwing the salt in each other's mugs, or pelting each other with bits of bread, or anything nice and entertaining, down came those merciless keepers on their innocent mirth, and the old stupid order went round for sitting upright and quiet. Nothing that I can say about it would be half as expressive as what the little Victims used to say themselves. They said that it was '*so very hard.*'

"Now, then, a good groan for the *dinner* misery," exclaimed Aunt Judy in conclusion.

The order was obeyed, but somewhat reluctantly, and then Aunt Judy proceeded with her tale.

"On one occasion of the *dinner* misery," resumed she, "there happened to be a stranger lady present, who seemed to be very much shocked by what the Victims had to undergo, and to pity them very much; so she said she would set them a nice little puzzle to amuse them till the second course arrived. But now, what do you think the puzzle was? It was a question, and this was it. 'Which is the harder thing to bear - to have to wait for your dinner, or to have no dinner to wait for?'

"I do not think the little Victims would have quite known what the stranger lady meant, if she had not explained herself; for you see *they* had never gone without dinner in their lives, so they had not an idea what sort of a feeling it was to have *no dinner to wait for*. But she went on to tell them what it was like as well as she could. She described to them little Tommy Brown, (whom they envied so much for having no lessons to do,) eating his potatoe soaked in the dripping begged at the squire's back-door, without anything else to wait - or hope for. She told them that *he* was never teazed as to how he sat, or even whether he sat or stood, and then she asked them if they did not think he was a very happy little boy? He had no trouble or bother, but just ate his rough morsel in any way he pleased, and then was off, hungry or not hungry, into the streets again.

"To tell you the truth," pursued Aunt Judy, "the Victims did not know what to say to the lady's account of little Tommy Brown's happiness; but as the roast meat came in just as it concluded, perhaps that diverted their attention. However, after they had all been helped, it was suddenly observed that one of them would not begin to eat. He sat with his head bent over his plate, and his cheeks growing redder and redder, till at last some one asked what was amiss, and why he would not go on with his dinner, on which he sobbed out that he had 'much rather it was taken to little Tommy Brown!'"

"That was a very *good* little Victim, wasn't he?" asked No. 8.

"But what did the keepers say?" inquired No. 5, rather anxiously.

"Oh," replied Aunt Judy, "it was soon settled that Tommy Brown was to have the dinner, which made the little Victim so happy, he actually jumped for joy. On which the stranger lady told them she hoped they would henceforth always ask themselves her curious question whenever they sat down to a good meal again. 'For,' said she, 'my dears, it will teach you to be thankful; and you may take my word for it, it is always the ungrateful people who are the most miserable ones.'"

"Oh, Aunt Judy!" here interposed No. 6, somewhat vehemently, "you need not tell any more! I know you mean *us* by the little Victims! But you don't think we really *mean* to be ungrateful about the beds, or the dinners, or anything, do you?"

There was a melancholy earnestness in the tone of the inquiry, which rather grieved Aunt Judy, for she knew it was not well to magnify childish faults into too great importance: so she took No. 6 on her knee, and assured her she never imagined such a thing as their being really ungrateful, for a moment. If she had, she added, she should not have turned their little ways into fun, as she had done in the story.

No. 6 was comforted somewhat on hearing this, but still leant her head on Aunt Judy's shoulder in a rather pensive state.

"I wonder what makes one so tiresome," mused the meditative No. 5, trying to view the matter quite abstractedly, as if he himself was in no way concerned in it.

"Thoughtlessness only," replied Aunt Judy, smiling. "I have often heard mamma say it is not ingratitude in *children* when they don't think about the comforts they enjoy every day; because the comforts seem to them to come, like air and sunshine, as a mere matter of course."

"Really?" exclaimed No. 6, in a quite hopeful tone. "Does mamma really say that?"

Yes; but then you know," continued Aunt Judy, "everybody has to be taught to think by degrees, and then they get to know that no comforts ever do really come to anybody as a matter of course. No, not even air and sunshine; but every one of them as blessings permitted by God, and which, therefore, we have to be thankful for. So you see we have to *learn* to be thankful as we have to learn everything else, and mamma says it is a lesson that never ends, even for grown-up people.

"And now you understand, No. 6, that you - oh! I beg pardon, I mean *the little Victims* - were not really ungrateful, but only thoughtless; and the wonderful stranger lady did something to cure them of that, and, in fact, proved a sort of Aunt Judy to them; for she explained things in such a very entertaining manner, that they actually began to think the matter over; and then they left off being stupid and unthankful.

"But this reminds me," added Aunt Judy, "that you - tiresome No. 6 - have spoilt my story after all! I had not half got to the end of the miseries. For instance, there was the *taking-care* misery, in consequence of which the little Victims were sent out to play on a fine day, and kept in when it was stormy and wet, all because those stupid keepers were more anxious to keep them well in health than to please them at the moment.

"And then there was - above all - " here Aunt Judy became very impressive, "the *washing* misery, which consisted in their being obliged to make themselves clean and comfortable with soap and water whenever they happened to be dirty, whether with playing at knuckle-bones on the floor, or anything else, and which was considered *so hard* that - "

But here a small hand was laid on Aunt Judy's mouth, and a gentle voice said, "Stop, Aunt Judy, now!" on which the rest shouted, "Stop! stop! we won't hear any more," in chorus, until all at once, in the midst of the din, there sounded outside the door the ominous knocking, which announced the hour of repose to the juvenile branches of the family.

It was a well-known summons, but on this occasion produced rather an unusual effect. First, there was a sudden profound silence, and pause of several seconds; then an interchange of glances among the little ones; then a breaking out of involuntary smiles upon several young faces; and at last a universal "Good-night, Aunt Judy!" very quietly and demurely spoken.

"If the little Victims were only here to see how *you* behave over the *going-to-bed* misery, what a lesson it would be!" suggested Aunt Judy, with a mischievous smile.

"Ah, yes, yes, we know, we know!" was the only reply, and it came from No. 8, who took advantage of being the youngest to be more saucy than the rest.

Aunt Judy now led the little party into the drawing-room to bid their father and mother good-night too. And certainly when the door was opened, and they saw how bright and cosy everything looked, in the light of the fire and the lamps, with mamma at the table, wide awake and smiling, they underwent a fearful twinge of the *going-to-bed* misery. But they checked all expression of their feelings. Of course, mamma asked what Aunt Judy's story had been about, and heard; and heard, too, No. 6's little trouble lest she should have been guilty of the sin of real ingratitude; and, of course, mamma applauded Aunt Judy's explanation about the want of thought, very much indeed.

"But, mamma," said No. 6 to her mother, "Aunt Judy said something about grown-up people having to learn to be thankful. Surely you and papa never cry for nonsense, and things you can't have?"

"Ah, my darling No. 6," cried mamma earnestly, "grown-up people may not *cry* for what they want exactly, but they are just as apt to wish for what they cannot have, as you little ones are. For instance, grown-up people would constantly like to have life made easier and more agreeable to them, than God chooses it to be. They would like to have a little more wealth, perhaps, or a little more health, or a little more

Mrs Alfred Gatty

rest, or that their children should always be good and clever, and well and happy. And while they are thinking and fretting about the things they want, they forget to be thankful for those they have. I am often tempted in this way myself, dear No. 6; so you see Aunt Judy is right, and the lesson of learning to be thankful never ends, even for grown-up people.

"One other word before you go. I dare say you little ones think we grown-up people are quite independent, and can do just as we like. But it is not so. We have to learn to submit to the will of the great Keeper of Heaven and earth, without understanding it, just as Aunt Judy's little Victims had to submit to their keepers without knowing why. So thank Aunt Judy for her story, and let us all do our best to be obedient and contented."

"When I am old enough, mother," remarked No. 7, in his peculiarly mild and deliberate way of speaking, and smiling all the time, "I think I shall put Aunt Judy into a story. Don't you think she would make a capital Ogre's wife, like the one in 'Jack and the Bean-Stalk,' who told Jack how to behave, and gave him good advice?"

It was a difficult question to say "No" to, so mamma kissed No. 7, instead of answering him, and No. 7 smiled himself away, with his head full of the bright idea.

VEGETABLES OUT OF PLACE.

But any man that walks the mead,
In bud or blade, or bloom, may find,
According as his humours lead,
A meaning suited to his mind."

TENNYSON.

It was a fine May morning. Not one of those with an east wind and a bright sun, which keep people in a puzzle all as day to whether it is hot or cold, and cause endless nursery disputes about the keeping on of comforters and warm coats, whenever a hoop-race, or some such active exertion, has brought a universal puggyness over the juvenile frame - but it was a really mild, sweet-scented day, when it is quite a treat to be out of doors, whether in the gardens, the lanes, or the fields, and when nothing but a holland jacket is thought necessary by even the most tiresomely careful of mammas.

It was not a day which anybody would have chosen to be poorly upon; but people have no choice in such matters, and poor little No. 7, of our old friends "the little ones," was in bed ill of the measles.

The wise old Bishop, Jeremy Taylor, told us long ago, how well children generally bear sickness. "They bear

Mrs Alfred Gatty

it," he says, "by a direct sufferance;" that is to say, they submit to just what discomfort exists at the moment, without fidgetting about either a cause or a consequence," and decidedly without fretting about what is to come.

For a grown-up person to attain to the same state of unanxious resignation, is one of the high triumphs of Christian faith. It is that "delivering one's self up," of which the poor speak so forcibly on their sick-beds.

No. 7 proved a charming instance of the truth of Jeremy Taylor's remark. He behaved in the most composed manner over his feelings, and even over his physic.

During the first day or two, when he sat shivering by the fire, reading "Neill D'Arcy's Life at Sea," and was asked how he felt, he answered with his usual smile; "Oh, all right; only a little cold now and then." And afterwards, when he was in bed in a darkened room, and the same question was put, he replied almost as quietly, (though without the smile,) "Oh - only a little too hot."

Then over the medicine, he contested nothing. He made, indeed, one or two by no means injudicious suggestions, as to the best method of having the disagreeable material, whether powdery or oleaginous, (I will not particularize further!) conveyed down his throat: commonly said, "Thank you," even before he had swallowed it; and then shut his eyes, and kept himself quiet.

Fortunately No. 1, and Schoolboy No. 3, had had the complaint as well as papa and mamma, so there were plenty to share in the nursing and house matters. The only question was, what was to be done with the little ones while Nurse was so busy; and Aunt Judy volunteered her services in their behalf.

Now it will easily be supposed, after what I have said, that the nursing was not at all a difficult undertaking; but I am grieved to say that Aunt Judy's task was by no means so easy a one.

The little ones were very sorry, it is true, that No. 7 was poorly; but, unluckily, they forgot it every time they went either up-stairs or down. They could not bear in their minds the fact, that when they encouraged the poodle to bark after an India-rubber ball, he was pretty sure to wake No. 7 out of a nap; and, in short, the day being so fine, and the little ones so noisy, Aunt Judy packed them all off into their gardens to tidy them up, she herself taking her station in a small study, the window of which looked out upon the family play-ground.

Her idea, perhaps, was, that she could in this way combine the prosecution of her own studies, with enacting policeman over the young gardeners, and "keeping the peace," as she called it. But if so, she was doomed to disappointment.

The operation of "tidying up gardens," as performed by a set of "little ones," scarcely needs description.

It consists of a number of alterations being thought of, and set about, not one of which is ever known to be finished by those who begin them. It consists of everybody wanting the rake at the same moment, and of nobody being willing to use the other tools, which they call stupid and useless things. It consists of a great many plants being moved from one place to another, when they are in full flower, and dying in consequence. (But how, except when they are in flower, can anyone judge where they will look best?) It consists of a great many seeds being prevented from coming up at all, by an "alteration" cutting into the heart of the patch just as they were bursting their shells for a sprout. It consists of an unlimited and fatal application of the cold-water cure.

And, finally, it results in such a confusion between foot-walks and beds - such a mixture of earth and gravel, and thrown-down tools - that anyone unused to the symptoms of the case, might imagine that the door of the pigsty in the yard had been left open, and that its inhabitant had been performing sundry uncouth gambols with his nose in the little ones' gardens.

Aunt Judy was quite aware of these facts, and she had accordingly laid down several rules, and given several instructions to prevent the usual catastrophe; and all went very smoothly at first in consequence. The little ones went out all hilarity and delight, and divided the tools with considerable show of justice, while Aunt Judy nodded to them approvingly out of her window, and then settled down to an interesting sum in that most peculiar of all arithmetical rules, "*The Rule of False*," the principle of which is, that out of two errors, made by yourself from two wrong guesses, you arrive at a discovery of the truth!

When Aunt Judy first caught sight of this rule, a few days before, at the end of an old summing-book, it struck her fancy at once. The principle of it was capable of a much more general application than to the

"Rule of False," and she amused herself by studying it up.

It is, no doubt, a clumsy substitute for algebra; but young folks who have not learnt algebra, will find it a very entertaining method of making out all such sums as the following old puzzler, over which Aunt Judy was now poring:

"There is a certain fish, whose head is 9 inches in length, his tail as long as his head and half of his back, and his back as long as both head and tail together. Query, the length of the fish?"

But Aunt Judy was not left long in peace with her fish. While she was in the thick of "suppositions" and "errors," a tap came at the window.

"Aunt Judy!"

"Stop!" was the answer; and the hand of the speaker went up, with the slate-pencil in it, enforcing silence while she pursued her calculations.

"Say, back 42 inches; then tail (half back) 21, and head given, 9, that's 30, and 30 and 9, 39 back. - Won't do! Second error: three inches - What's the matter, No. 6? You surely have not begun to quarrel already?"

"Oh, no," answered No. 6, with her nose flattened against the window-pane. "But please, Aunt Judy, No. 8 won't have the oyster-shell trimming round his garden any longer, he says; he says it looks so rubbishy. But as my garden joins his down the middle, if he takes away the oyster-shells all round his, then one of *my* sides - the one in the middle, I mean - will be left bare, don't you see? and I want to keep the oyster-shells all round may garden, because mamma says there are still some zoophytes upon them. So how is it to be?"

What a perplexity! The fish with his nine-inch head, and his tail as long as his head and half of his back, was a mere nothing to it.

Aunt Judy threw open the window.

"My dear No. 6," answered she, "yours is the great boundary-line question about which nations never do agree, but go squabbling on till some one has to give way first. There is but one plan for settling it, and that is, for each of you to give up a piece of your gardens to make a road to run between. Now if you'll both give way at once, and consent to this, I will come out to you myself, and leave my fish till the evening. It's much too fine to stay in doors, I feel; and I can give you all something real to do."

"*I'll* give way, I'm sure, Aunt Judy," cried No. 6, quite glad to be rid of the dispute; "and so will you, won't you, No. 8?" she added, appealing to that young gentleman, who stood with his pinafore full of dirty oyster-shells, not quite understanding the meaning of what was said.

"I'll *what*?" inquired he.

"Oh, never mind! Only throw the oyster-shells down, and come with Aunt Judy. It will be much better fun than staying here."

No. 8 lowered his pinafore at the word of command,

and dropped the discarded oyster-shells, one by one - where do you think? - why - right into the middle of his little garden! an operation which seemed to be particularly agreeable to him, if one might judge by his face. He was not sorry either to be relieved from the weight.

"You see, Aunt Judy," continued No. 6 to her sister, who had now joined them, "it doesn't so much matter about the oyster-shell trimming; but No. 8's garden is always in such a mess, that I must have a wall or something between us!"

"You shall have a wall or a path decidedly," replied Aunt Judy: "a road is the next best thing to a river for a boundary-line. But now, all of you, pick up the tools and come with me, and you shall do some regular work, and be paid for it at the rate of half-a-farthing for every half hour. Think what a magnificent offer!"

The little ones thought so in reality, and welcomed the arrangement with delight, and trudged off behind Aunt Judy, calculating so hard among themselves what their conjoint half-farthings would come to, for the half-hours they all intended to work, and furthermore, what amount or variety of "goodies" they would purchase, that Aunt Judy half fancied herself back in the depths of the "Rule of False" again!

She led them at last to a pretty shrubbery-walk, of which they were all very fond. On one side of it was a quick-set hedge, in which the honeysuckle was mixed so profusely with the thorn, that they grew and were clipped together.

It was the choicest spot for a quiet evening stroll in

Mrs Alfred Gatty

summer that could possibly be imagined. The sweet scent from the honeysuckle flowers stole around you with a welcome as you moved along, and set you a dreaming of some far-off region where the delicious sensations produced by the odour of flowers may not be as transient as they are here.

There was an alcove in the middle of the walk - not one of the modern mockeries of rusticity - but a real old-fashioned lath-and-plaster concern, such as used to be erected in front of a bowling-green. It was roofed in, was open only on the sunny side, and was supported by a couple of little Ionic pillars, up which clematis and passion-flower were studiously trained.

There was a table as well as seats within; and the alcove was a very nice place for either reading or drawing in, as it commanded a pretty view of the distant country. It was also, and perhaps especially, suited to the young people in their more poetical and fanciful moods.

The little ones had no sooner reached the entrance of the favourite walk, than they scampered past Aunt Judy to run a race; but No. 6 stopped suddenly short.

"Aunt Judy, look at these horrible weeds! Ah! I do believe this is what you have brought us here for!"

It was indeed; for some showers the evening before, had caused them to flourish in a painfully prominent manner, and the favourite walk presented a somewhat neglected appearance.

So Aunt Judy marked it off for the little ones to weed, repeated the exhilarating promise of the half-farthings, and seated herself in the alcove to puzzle out the length of the fish.

At first it was rather amusing to hear, how even in the midst of their weeding, the little ones pursued their calculations of the anticipated half-farthings, and discussed the niceness and prices of the various descriptions of "goodies."

But by degrees, less and less was said; and at last, the half-farthings and "goodies" seemed altogether forgotten, and a new idea to arise in their place.

The new idea was, that this weeding-task was uncommonly troublesome!

"I'm sure there are many more weeds in my piece than in anybody else's!" remarked the tallest of the children, standing up to rest his rather tired back, and contemplate the walk. "I don't think Aunt Judy measured it out fair!"

"Well, but you're the biggest, and ought to do the most," responded No. 6.

"A *little* the most is all very well," persisted No. 5; "but I've got *too much* the most rather - and it's very tiresome work."

"What nonsense!" rejoined No. 6. "I don't believe the weeds are any thicker in your piece than in mine. Look at my big heap. And I'm sure I'm quite as tired as you are."

No. 6 got up as she spoke, to see how matters were going on; not at all sorry either, to change her position.

Mrs Alfred Gatty

"*I've* got the most," muttered No. 8 to himself, still kneeling over his work.

But this was, it is to be feared, a very unjustifiable bit of brag.

"If you go on talking so much, you will not get any half-farthings at all!" shouted No. 4, from the distance.

A pause followed this warning, and the small party ducked down again to their work.

They no longer liked it, however; and very soon afterwards the jocose No. 5 observed, in subdued tones to the others:-

"I wonder what *the little victims* would have said to this kind of thing?"

"They'd have hated it," answered No. 6, very decidedly.

The fact was, the little ones were getting really tired, for the fine May morning had turned into a hot day; and in a few minutes more, a still further aggravation of feeling took place.

No. 6 got up again, shook the gravel from her frock, blew it off her hands, pushed back a heap of heavy curls from her face, set her hat as far back on her head as she could, and exclaimed:-

"I wish there were no such things as weeds in the world!"

Everybody seemed struck with this impressive

sentiment, for they all left off weeding at once, and Aunt Judy came forward to the front of the alcove.

"Don't you, Aunt Judy?" added No. 6, feeling sure her sister had heard.

"Not I, indeed," answered Aunt Judy, with a comical smile: "I'm too fond of cream to my tea."

"Cream to your tea, Aunt Judy? What can that have to do with it?"

The little ones were amazed.

"Something," at any rate, responded Aunt Judy; "and if you like to come in here, and sit down, I will tell you how."

Away went hoes and weeding-knives at once, and into the alcove they rushed; and never had garden-seats felt so thoroughly comfortable before.

"If one begins to wish," suggested No. 5, stretching his legs out to their full extent, "one may as well wish oneself a grand person with a lot of gardeners to clear away the weeds as fast as they come up, and save one the trouble."

"Much better wish them away, and save everybody the trouble," persisted No. 6.

"No: one wants them sometimes."

"What an idea! Who ever wants weeds?"

"You yourself."

"I? What nonsense!"

But the persevering No. 5 proceeded to explain. No. 6 had asked him a few days before to bring her some groundsel for her canary, and he had been quite disappointed at finding none in the garden. He had actually to "trail" into the lanes to fetch a bit.

This was a puzzling statement; so No. 6 contented herself with grumbling out:-

"Weeds are welcome to grow in the lanes."

"Weeds are not always weeds in the lanes," persisted No. 5, with a grin: "they're sometimes wild-flowers."

"I don't care what they are," pouted No. 6. "I wish I lived in a place where there were none."

"And I wish I was a great man, with lots of gardeners to take them up, instead of me," maintained No. 5, who was in a mood of lazy tiresomeness, and kept rocking to and fro on the garden-chair, with his hands tucked under his thighs. "A weed - a weed," continued he; "what is a weed, I wonder? Aunt Judy, what is a weed?"

Aunt Judy had surely been either dreaming or cogitating during the last few minutes, for she had taken no notice of what was said, but she roused up now, and answered:-

"A vegetable out of its place."

"A *vegetable*," repeated No. 5, "why we don't eat them, Aunt Judy."

"You kitchen-garden interpreter, who said we did?" replied she. "All green herbs are *vegetables,* let me tell you, whether we eat them or not."

"Oh, I see," mused No. 5, quietly enough, but in another instant he broke out again.

"I'll tell you what though, some of them are real vegetables, I mean kitchen-garden vegetables, to other creatures, and that's why they're wanted. Groundsel's a vegetable, it's the canary's vegetable. I mean his kitchen-garden vegetable, and if he had a kitchen-garden of his own, he would grow it as we do peas. So I was right after all, No. 6!"

That *twit* at the end spoilt everything, otherwise this was really a bright idea of No. 5's.

"Aunt Judy, do begin to talk yourself," entreated No. 6. "I wish No. 5 would be quiet, and not teaze."

"And he wishes the same of you," replied Aunt Judy, "and I wish the same of you all. What is to be done? Come, I will tell you a story, on one positive under-standing, namely, that whoever teazes, or even *twits,* shall be turned out of the company."

No. 5 sat up in his chair like a dart in an instant, and vowed that he would be the best of the good, till Aunt Judy had finished her story.

"After which - " concluded he, with a wink and another grin.

"After which, I shall expect you to be better still," was Aunt Judy's emphatic rejoinder. And peace being now completely established, she commenced: "There was once upon a time - what do you think?" - here she paused and looked round in the children's faces.

"A giant!" exclaimed No. 8.

"A beautiful princess!" suggested No. 6.

"*Something*," said Aunt Judy, "but I am not going to tell you what at present. You must find out for yourselves. Meantime I shall call it *something*, or merely make a grunting - hm - when I allude to it, as people do to express a blank."

The little ones shuffled about in delighted impatience at the notion of the mysterious "something" which they were to find out, and Aunt Judy proceeded:-

"This - hm - then, lived in a large meadow field, where it was the delight of all beholders. The owner of the property was constantly boasting about it to his friends, for he maintained that it was the richest, and most beautiful, and most valuable - hm - in all the country round. Surely no other thing in this world ever found itself more admired or prized than this *something* did. The commonest passer-by would notice it, and say all manner of fine things in its praise, whether in the early spring, the full summer, or the autumn, for at each of these seasons it put on a fresh charm, and formed a subject of conversation. 'Only look at that lovely - hm - ' was quite a common exclamation at the sight of it. 'What a colour it has! How fresh and healthy it looks! How invaluable it must be! Why, it must be worth at least - ' and then the speaker would go calculating away at the number of pounds, shillings, and pence, the - hm - would fetch, if put into the money-market, which is, I am sorry to say, a very usual, although very degrading way of estimating worth.

"To conclude, the mild-eyed Alderney cow, who pastured in the field during the autumn months, would chew the cud of approbation over the - hm - for hours together, and people said it was no wonder at all that she gave such delicious milk and cream."

Here a shout of supposed discovery broke from No. 5. "I've guessed, I know it!"

But a "hush" from Aunt Judy stopped him short.

"No. 5, nobody asked your opinion, keep it to yourself, if you please."

No. 5 was silenced, but rubbed his hands nevertheless.

"Well," continued Aunt Judy, "that '*something*' ought surely to have been the most contented thing in the world. Its merits were acknowledged; its usefulness was undoubted; its beauty was the theme of constant admiration; what had it left to wish for? Really nothing; but by an unlucky accident it became dissatisfied with its situation in a meadow field, and wished to get into a higher position in life, which, it took for granted, would be more suited to its many exalted qualities. The '*something*' of the field wanted to inhabit a garden. The unlucky accident that gave rise to this foolish idea, was as follows:-

"A little boy was running across the beautiful meadow one morning, with a tin-pot full of fishing bait in his hand, when suddenly he stumbled and fell down.

Mrs Alfred Gatty

"The bait in the tin-pot was some lob-worms, which the little boy had collected out of the garden adjoining the field, and they were spilt and scattered about by his fall.

"He picked up as many as he could find, however, and ran off again; but one escaped his notice and was left behind.

"This gentleman was insensible for a few seconds; but as soon as he came to himself, and discovered that he was in a strange place, he began to grumble and find fault.

"'What an uncouth neighbourhood!' Such were his exclamations. 'What rough impracticable roads! Was ever lob-worm so unlucky before!' It was impossible to move an inch without bumping his sides against some piece of uncultivated ground.

"Judge for yourselves, my dears," continued Aunt Judy, pathetically, "what must have been the feelings of the '*something*' which had lived proudly and happily in the meadow field for so long, on hearing such offensive remarks.

"Its spirit was up in a minute, just as yours would have been, and it did not hesitate to inform the intruder that travellers who find fault with a country before they have taken the trouble to inquire into its merits, are very ignorant and impertinent people.

"This was blow for blow, as you perceive; and the *teaze-and-twit* system was now continued with great animation on both sides.

"The lob-worm inquired, with a conceited wriggle, what could be the merits of a country, where gentlemanly, gliding, thin-skinned creatures like himself were unable to move about without personal annoyance? Whereupon the amiable '*something*' made no scruple of telling the lob-worm that his *betters* found no fault with the place, and instanced its friend and admirer the Alderney cow.

"On which the lob-worm affected forgetfulness, and exclaimed, 'Cow? cow? do I know the creature? Ah! Yes, I recollect now; clumsy legs, horny feet, and that sort of thing,' proceeding to hint that what was good enough for a cow, might yet not be refined enough for his own more delicate habits.

"'It is my misfortune, perhaps,' concluded he, with mock humility, 'to have been accustomed to higher associations; but really, situated as I am here, I could almost feel disposed to - why, positively, to wish myself a cow, with clumsy legs and horny feet. What one may live to come to, to be sure!'

"Well," Aunt Judy proceeded, "will you believe it, the lob-worm went on boasting till the poor deluded '*something*' believed every word he said, and at last ventured to ask in what favoured spot he had acquired his superior tastes and knowledge.

"And then, of course, the lob-worm had the opportunity of opening out in a very magnificent bit of brag, and did not fail to do so.

"Travellers can always boast with impunity to stationary folk, and the lob-worm had no conscience about speaking the truth.

Mrs Alfred Gatty

So on he chattered, giving the most splendid account of the garden in which he lived. Gorgeous flowers, velvet lawns, polished gravel-walks, along which he was wont to take his early morning stroll, before the ruder creatures of the neighbourhood, such as dogs, cats, &c. were up and about, were all his discourse; and he spoke of them as if they were his own, and told of the nursing and tending of every plant in the lovely spot, as if the gardeners did it all for his convenience and pleasure.

"Of the little accidents to which he and his race have from time immemorial been liable from awkward spades, or those very early birds, by whom he ran a risk of being snapped up every time he emerged out of the velvet lawns for the morning strolls, he said just nothing at all.

"All was unmixed delight (according to his account) in the garden, and having actually boasted himself into good humour with himself, and therefore with everybody else, he concluded by expressing the condescending wish, that the 'something' in the field should get itself removed to the garden, to enjoy the life of which he spoke.

"'Undeniably beautiful as you are here,' cried he, 'your beauty will increase a thousand fold, under the gardener's fostering care. Appreciated as you are now in your rustic life, the most prominent place will be assigned to you when you get into more distinguished society; so that everybody who passes by and sees you, will exclaim in delight, 'Behold this exquisite - hm - !'"

"Oh dear, Aunt Judy," cried No. 6, "was the 'hum,' as

you will call it, so silly as to believe what he said?"

"How could the poor simple-minded thing be expected to resist such elegant compliments, my dear No. 6?" answered Aunt Judy. "But then came the difficulty. The *'something'* which lived in the field had no more legs than the lob-worm himself, and, in fact, was incapable of locomotion."

"Of course it was!" ejaculated No. 5.

"Order!" cried Aunt Judy, and proceeded:-

"So the - hm - hung down its graceful head in despair, but suddenly a bright and loving thought struck it. It could not change its place and rise in life itself, but its children might, and that would be some consolation. It opened its heart on this point to the lob-worm, and although the lob-worm had no heart to be touched, he had still a tongue to talk.

"If the - hm - would send its children to the garden at the first opportunity, he would be delighted, absolutely charmed, to introduce them in the world. He would put them in the way of everything, and see that they were properly attended to. There was nothing he couldn't or wouldn't do.

"This last pretentious brag seemed to have exhausted even the lob-worm's ingenuity, for, soon after he had uttered it, he shuffled away out of the meadow in the best fashion that he could, leaving the *'something'* in the field in a state of wondering regret. But it recovered its spirits again when the time came for sending its children to the favoured garden abode.

"'My dears,' it said, 'you will soon have to begin life for yourselves, and I hope you will do so with credit to your bringing up. I hope you are now ambitious enough to despise the dull old plan of dropping contentedly down, just where you happen to be, or waiting for some chance traveller (who may never come) to give you a lift elsewhere. That paradise of happiness, of which the lob-worm told us, is close at hand. Come! it only wants a little extra exertion on your part, and you will be carried thither by the wind, as easily as the wandering Dandelion himself. Courage, my dears! nothing out of the common is ever gained without an effort. See now! as soon as ever a strong breeze blows the proper way, I shall shake my heads as hard as ever I can, that you may be off. All the doors and windows are open now, you know, and you must throw yourselves out upon the wind. Only remember one thing, when you are settled down in the beautiful garden, mind you hold up your heads, and do yourselves justice, my dears.'

"The children gave a ready assent, of course, as proud as possible at the notion; and when the favourable breeze came, and the maternal heads were shaken, out they all flew, and trusted themselves to its guidance, and in a few minutes settled down all over the beautiful garden, some on the beds, some on the lawn, some on the polished gravel-walks. And all I can say is, happiest those who were least seen!"

"Grass weeds! grass weeds!" shouted the incorrigible No. 5, jumping up from his seat and performing two or three Dervish-like turns.

"Oh, it's too bad, isn't it, Aunt Judy," cried No. 6, "to stop your story in the middle?"

Whereupon Aunt Judy answered that he had not stopped the story in the middle, but at the end, and she was glad he had found out the meaning of her - *hm* - !

But No. 6 would not be satisfied, she liked to hear the complete finish up of everything. "Did the *'hum's'* children ever grow up in the garden, and did they ever see the lob-worm again?"

"The - hm's - children did *spring* up in the garden," answered Aunt Judy, "and did their best to exhibit their beauty on the polished gravel-walks, where they were particularly delighted with their own appearance one May morning after a shower of rain, which had made them more prominent than usual. 'Remember our mother's advice,' cried they to each other. 'This is the happy moment! Let us hold up our heads, and do ourselves justice, my dears.'

"Scarcely were the words spoken, when a troop of rude creatures came scampering into the walk, and a particularly unfeeling monster in curls, pointed to the beautiful up-standing little - hms - and shouted, 'Aunt Judy, look at these *horrible weeds*!'

"I needn't say any more," concluded Aunt Judy. "You know how you've used them; you know what you've done to them; you know how you've even wished there were *no such things in the world*!"

"Oh, Aunt Judy, how capital!" ejaculated No. 6, with a sigh, the sigh of exhausted amusement.

"'The *hum* was a weed too, then, was it?" said No. 8. He did not quite see his way through the tale.

Mrs Alfred Gatty

"It was not a weed in the meadow," answered Aunt Judy, "where it was useful, and fed the Alderney cow. It was beautiful Grass there, and was counted as such, because that was its proper place. But when it put its nose into garden-walks, where it was not wanted, and had no business, then everybody called the beautiful Grass a weed."

"So a weed is a vegetable out of its place, you see," subjoined No. 5, who felt the idea to be half his own, "and it won't do to wish there were none in the world."

"And a vegetable out of its place being nothing better than a weed, Mr. No. 5," added Aunt Judy, "it won't do to be too anxious about what is so often falsely called, bettering your condition in life. Come, the story is done, and now we'll go home, and all the patient listeners and weeders may reckon upon getting one or more farthings apiece from mamma. And as No. 6's wish is not realized, and there are still weeds {1} in the world, and among them Grass weeds, *I* shall hope to have some cream to my tea."

COOK STORIES.

"Down too, down at your own fireside,
With the evil tongue and the evil ear,
For each is at war with mankind."

          TENNYSON'S Maud.

Aunt Judy had gone to the nursery wardrobe to look over some clothes, and the little ones were having a play to themselves. As she opened the door, they were just coming to the end of an explosive burst of laughter, in which all the five appeared to have joined, and which they had some difficulty in stopping. No. 4, who was a biggish girl, had giggled till the tears were running over her cheeks; and No. 8, in sympathy, was leaning back in his tiny chair in a sort of ecstasy of amusement.

The five little ones had certainly hit upon some very entertaining game.

They were all (boys and girls alike) dressed up as elderly ladies, with bits of rubbishy finery on their heads and round their shoulders, to imitate caps and scarfs; the boys' hair being neatly parted and brushed down the middle; and they were seated in form round what was called "the Doll's Table," a concern just large enough to allow of a small crockery tea-service, with cups and saucers and little plates, being set out upon it.

"What have you got there?" was all Aunt Judy asked, as she went up to the table to look at them.

"Cowslip-tea," was No. 4's answer, laying her hand on the fat pink tea-pot; and thereupon the laughing explosion went off nearly as loudly as before, though for no accountable reason that Aunt Judy could divine.

"It's *so* good, Aunt Judy, do taste it!" exclaimed No. 8, jumping up in a great fuss, and holding up his little cup, full of a pale-buff fluid, to Aunt Judy.

"You'll have everything over," cried No. 4, calling him to order; and in truth the table was not the steadiest in the world.

So No. 8 sat down again, calling out, in an almost stuttering hurry, "You may keep it all, Aunt Judy, I don't want any more."

But neither did Aunt Judy, after she had given it one taste; so she put the cup down, thanking No. 8 very much, but pulling such a funny face, that it set the laugh going once more; in the middle of which No. 4 dropped an additional lump of sugar into the rejected buff-coloured mixture, a proceeding which evidently gave No. 8 a new relish for the beverage.

Aunt Judy had got beyond the age when cowslip-tea was looked upon as one of the treats of life; and she had not, on the other hand, lived long enough to love the taste of it for the memory's sake of the enjoyment it once afforded.

Not but what we are obliged to admit that cowslip-tea is one of those things which, even in the most enthusiastic days of youth, just falls short of the absolute perfection one expects from it.

Even under those most favourable circumstances of having had the delightful gathering of the flowers in the sweet sunny fields - the picking of them in the happy holiday afternoon - the permission to use the best doll's tea-service for the feast - the loan of a nice white table-cloth - and the present of half-a-dozen pewter knives and forks to fancy-cut the biscuits with - nay, even in spite of the addition of well-filled doll's sugar-pots and cream-jugs - cowslip-tea always seems to want either a leetle more or a leetle less sugar - or a leetle more or a leetle less cream - or to be a leetle more or a leetle less strong - to turn it into that complete nectar which, of course, it really *is*.

On the present occasion, however, the children had clearly got hold of some other source of enjoyment over the annual cowslip-tea feast, besides the beverage itself; and Aunt Judy, glad to see them so safely happy, went off to her business at the wardrobe, while the little ones resumed their game.

"Very extraordinary, indeed, ma'am!" began one of the fancy old ladies, in a completely fancy voice, a little affected, or so. "*Most* extraordinary, ma'am, I may say!"

(Here there was a renewed giggle from No. 4, which she carefully smothered in her handkerchief.)

"But still I think I can tell you of something more extraordinary still!"

The speaker having at this point refreshed his ideas by a sip of the pale-coloured tea, and the other ladies having laughed heartily in anticipation of the fun that was coming, one of them observed:-

"You don't *say* so, ma'am - " then clicked astonishment with her tongue against the roof of her mouth several times, and added impressively, "*Pray* let us hear!"

"I shall be most happy, ma'am," resumed the first speaker, with a graceful inclination forwards. "Well! - you see - it was a party. I had invited some of my most distinguished friends - really, ma'am, *fashionable* friends, I may say, to dinner; and, ahem! you see - some little anxiety always attends such affairs - even - in the best regulated families!"

Here the speaker winked considerably at No. 4, and laughed very loudly himself at his own joke.

"Dear me, you must excuse me, ma'am," he proceeded. "So, you see, I felt a little fatigued by my morning's exertions, (to tell you the truth, there had been no end of bother about everything!) and I retired quietly up-stairs to take a short nap before the dressing-bell rang. But I had not been laid down quite half an hour, when there was a loud knock at the door. Really, ma'am, I felt quite alarmed, but was just able to ask, 'Who's there?' Before I had time to get an answer, however, the door was burst open by the housemaid. Her face was absolute scarlet, and she sobbed out:-

"'Oh, ma'am, what shall we do?'

"'Good gracious, Hannah,' cried I, 'what can be the matter? Has the soot come down the chimney? Speak!'

"'It's nothing of that sort, ma'am,' answered Hannah, 'it's the cook!'

"'The cook!' I shouted. 'I wish you would not be so foolish, Hannah, but speak out at once. What about Cook?'

"'Please, m'm, the cook's lost!' says Hannah. 'We can't find her!'

"'Your wits are lost, Hannah, *I* think,' cried I, and sent her to tidy the rooms while I slipt downstairs to look for the cook.

"Fancy a lost cook, ma'am! Was there ever such a ridiculous idea? And on the day of a dinner-party too! Did you ever hear of such a trial to a lady's feelings before?"

"Never, I am sure," responded the lady opposite. "Did *you,* ma'am?" turning to her neighbour.

But the other three ladies all shook their heads, bit their lips, and declared that they "Never had, they were sure!"

"I thought not!" ejaculated the narrator. "Well, ma'am, I went into the kitchens, the larder, the pantries, the cellars, and all sorts of places, and still no cook! Do you know, she really was nowhere! Actually, ma'am, the cook was lost!"

Mrs Alfred Gatty

Shouts of laughter burst forth here; but the lady (who was No. 5) put up his hand, and called out in his own natural tones:-

"Stop! I haven't got to the end yet!"

"Order!" proclaimed No. 4 immediately, in a very commanding voice, and thumping the table with the head of an old wooden doll to enforce obedience.

And then the sham lady proceeded in the same mincing voice as before:-

"Well! - dear me, I'm quite put out. But however, you see - what was to be done, that was the thing. It wanted only half an hour to dinner-time, and there was the meat roasting away by itself, and the potatoe-pan boiling over. You never heard such a fizzling as it made in your life - in short, everything was in a mess, and there was no cook.

"Well! I basted the meat for a few minutes, took the potatoe-pan off the fire, and then ran up-stairs to put on my bonnet. Thought I, the best thing I can do is to send somebody for the policeman, and let *him* find the cook. But while I was tying the strings of my bonnet, I fancied I heard a mysterious noise coming out of the bottom drawer of my wardrobe. Fancy that, ma'am, with my nerves in such a state from the cook being lost!"

No. 5 paused, and looked round for sympathy, which was most freely given by the other ladies, in the shape of sighs and exclamations.

"The drawer was a very deep drawer, ma'am, so I

thought perhaps the cat had crept in," continued No. 5. "Well, I went to it to see, and there it was, partly open, with a cotton gown in it that didn't belong to me. Imagine my feelings at *that,* ma'am! So I pulled at the handles to get the drawer quite open, but it wouldn't come, it was as heavy as lead. It was really very alarming - one doesn't like such odd things happening - but at last I got it open, though I tumbled backwards as I did so; and what do you think, ma'am - ladies - what *do* you think was in it?"

"The cook!" shrieked No. 4, convulsed with laughter; and the whole party clapped their hands and roared applause.

"The cook, ma'am, actually the cook!" pursued No. 5, "one of the fattest, most *poonchy* little women you ever saw. And what do you think was the history of it? I kept my up-stairs Pickwick in the corner of that bottom drawer. She had seen it there that very morning, when she was helping to dust the room, and took the opportunity of a spare half-hour to slip up and rest herself by reading it in the drawer. Unluckily, however, she had fallen asleep, and when I got the drawer out, there she lay, and I actually heard her snore. A shocking thing this education, ma'am, you see, and teaching people to read. All the cooks in the country are spoilt!"

Peals of laughter greeted this wonderfully witty concoction of No. 5's, and the lemon-coloured tea and biscuits were partaken of during the pause which followed.

Aunt Judy meanwhile, who had been quite unable to resist joining in the laugh herself, was seated on the floor, behind the open door of the wardrobe, thinking to herself of certain passages in Wordsworth's most beautiful ode, in which he has described the play of children,

> "As if their whole vocation
> Were endless imitation."

Truly they had got hold here of strange

"Fragments from their dream of human life."

Where *could* the children have picked up the original of such absurd nonsense?

Aunt Judy had no time to make it out, for now the mincing voices began again, and she sat listening.

"Have *you* had no curious adventures with your maids, ma'am?" inquires No. 5 of No. 4.

No. 5 makes an attempt at a bewitching grin as he speaks, fanning himself with a fan which he has had in his hand all the time he was telling his story.

"Well, ladies," replied No. 4, only just able to compose herself to talk, "I don't think I *have* been quite as fortunate as yourselves in having so many extra-ordinary things to tell. My servants have been sadly common-place, and done just as they ought. But still, *once,* ladies - once, a curious little incident did occur to me."

"Oh, ma'am, I entreat you - pray let us hear it!" burst from all the ladies at once.

No. 4 had to bite her lip to preserve her gravity, and then she turned to No. 5 –

"The fan, if you please, ma'am!"

The rule was, that the one fan was placed at the disposal of the story-teller for the time, so No. 5 handed it to No. 4, with a graceful bow; and No. 4 waffed it to and fro immediately, and began her account:-

"People are so unscrupulous you see, ladies, about giving characters. It's really shocking. For my part, I don't know what the world will come to at last. We shall all have to be our own servants, I suppose. People say anything about anything, that's the fact! Only fancy, ma'am, three different ladies once recommended a cook to me as the best soup-maker in the country. Now that sounded a very high recommen-dation, for, of course, if a cook can make soups, she can do anything - sweetmeats and those kind of things follow of themselves. So, ma am, I took her, and had a dinner-party, and ordered two soups, entirely that I might show off what a good cook I had got. Think what a compliment to her, and how much obliged she ought to have been! Well, ma'am, I ordered the two soups, as I said, one white, and the other brown; and everything appeared to be going on in the best possible manner, when, as I was sitting in the drawing-room entertaining the company, I was told I was wanted.

"When I got out of the room, there was the man I had hired to wait, and says he:-

"'If you please, ma'am where are the knives? I can't find any at all!'

"'No knives!' says I. 'Dear me, don't come to me about the knives. Ask the cook, of course.'

"'Please, ma'am, I have asked her, and she only laughed.'

"'Then,' said I, 'ask the housemaid. It's impossible for me to come out and look for the knives.'

"Well, ladies," continued No. 4, "would you believe it? - could anyone believe it? - when I sat down to dinner, and began to help the soup, no sooner had the silver ladle (*my* ladle is silver, ladies) been plunged into the tureen, than a most singular rattling was heard.

"'William,' cried I, half in a whisper, to the waiter who was holding the plate, 'what in the world is this? Surely Cook has not left the bones in?'

"'Please, ma'am, I don't know,' was all the man could say.

"Well - there was no remedy now, so I dipped the ladle in again, and lifted out - oh! ma'am, I know if it was anybody but myself who told you, you wouldn't believe it - a ladleful of the lost knives! There they were, my best beautiful ivory handles, all in the white soup! And while I was discovering them, the gentleman at the other end of the table had found all the kitchen-knives, with black handles, in the brown soup!

"There never was anything so mortifying before. And what do you think was Cook's excuse, when I reproached her?

"'Please, ma'am,' said she, 'I read in the *Young Woman's Vademecum of Instructive Information,* page 150, that there was nothing in the world so strengthening and wholesome as dissolved bones, and ivory-dust; and so, ma'am, I always make a point of throwing in a few knives into every soup I have the charge of, for the sake of the handles - ivory-handles for white soups, ma'am, and black-handles for the browns!'"

Thunders of applause interrupted Cook's excuse at this point, and No. 7 was so overcome that he pushed his chair back, and performed three distinct somersets on the floor, to the complete disorganization of his head-dress, which consisted of a turban, from beneath which hung a cluster of false curls.

Turban and wig being replaced, however, and No. 7 reseated and composed, No. 4 proceeded:-

"Cook generally takes them out, she informed me, ladies, before the tureens come to table; 'but,' said she, 'my back was turned for a minute here, ma'am, and that stupid William carried them off without asking if they were ready. It's all William's fault, ma'am; and I don't mean to stay, for I don't like a place where the man who waits has no tact!'

"Now, ladies," continued No. 4, "what do you think of that by way of a speech from a cook? And I assure you that a medical man's wife, to whom I mentioned in the course of the evening what Cook had said about dissolved bones, told me that her husband had only laughed, and said Cook was quite right. So she hired the woman that night herself, and I have been told in confidence since - you'll not repeat it, therefore, of course, ladies?"

"Of course not!" came from all sides.

"Well, then, I was told that, before the year was out, the family hadn't a knife that would cut anything, they were so cankered with rust. So much for education and learning to read, as you justly observed, ma'am, before!"

When the emotions produced by this tale had a little subsided, No. 7 was called upon for his experience of maids.

No. 7, with the turban on his head, and a fine red necklace round his throat, said he took very little notice of the maids, but that he once had had a very tiresome little boy in buttons, who was extremely fond of sugar, and always carried the sugar-shaker in his pocket, and ate up the sugar that was in it, and when it was empty, filled it up with magnesia.

"But *once*," he added, "ladies, he actually put some soda in. It was at a party, and we had our first rhubarb tart for the season, and the company sprinkled it all over with the soda and began to eat, but they were too polite to say how nasty it was. But, of course, when I was helped I called out. And what do you think the boy in buttons said?"

Nobody could guess, so No. 7 had to tell them.

"He said he had put it in on purpose, because he thought it would correct the acid of the pie. So I said he had best be apprenticed to a doctor; so he went - I dare say, ma'am, it was the same doctor who took your cook - but I never heard of him any more, and I've never dared to have a boy in buttons again."

"A very wise decision, ma'am, I'm sure!" cried Aunt Judy, who came up to the wonderful tea-table in the midst of the last mound of applause. "And now may I ask what game this is that you are playing at?"

"Oh, we're telling *Cook Stories,* Aunt Judy," cried No. 6, seizing her by the arm; "they're such capital fun! I wish you had heard mine; they were laughing at it when you first came in!"

"It must have been delicious, to judge by the delight it gave," replied Aunt Judy, smiling, and kissing No. 6's oddly bedizened up-turned face. "But what I want to know is, what put Cook Stories, as you call them, into your head?"

"Oh! don't you remember - " and here followed a long account from No. 6 of how, about a week before, the little ones had gone somewhere to spend the day, and how it had turned out a very rainy day, so that they could not have games out of doors with their young friends, as had been expected, but were obliged to sit a great part of the time in the drawing-room, putting Chinese puzzles together into stupid patterns, and playing at fox-and-goose, while the ladies were talking "grown-up conversation," as No. 6 worded it, among themselves; and, of course, being on their own good behaviour, and very quiet, they could not help hearing what was said. "And, oh dear, Aunt Judy," continued No. 6, now with both her arms holding Aunt Judy, of whom she was very fond, (except at lesson times!) round the waist, "it was so odd! No. 7 and I did nothing at last but listen and watch them; for little

Miss, who sat with us, was shy, and wouldn't talk, and it was so very funny to see the ladies nodding and making faces at each other, and whispering, and exclaiming, how shocking! how abominable! you don't say so! and all that kind of thing!"

"Well, but what was shocking, and abominable, and all that kind of thing?" inquired Aunt Judy.

"Oh, I don't know - things the nurses, and cooks, and boys in buttons did. Almost all the ladies had some story to tell - all the servants had done something or other queer - but especially the cooks, Aunt Judy, there was no end to the cooks. So one day after we came back, and we didn't know what to play at, I said: 'Do let us play at telling Cook Stories, like the ladies at -- .' So we've dressed up, and played at Cook Stories, ever since. Dear Aunt Judy, I wish you would invent a Cook Story yourself!" was the conclusion of No. 6's account.

So then the mystery was out. Aunt Judy's wonderings were cut short. Out of the real life of civilized intelligent society had come those

"Fragments from their dream of human life,"

which Aunt Judy had called absurd nonsense. And absurd nonsense, indeed, it was; but Aunt Judy was seized by the idea that some good might be got out of it.

So, in answer to No. 6's wish, she said, with a shy smile:-

"I don't think I could tell Cook Stories half as well as

yourself. But if, by way of a change, you would like a *Lady* Story instead, perhaps I might be able to accomplish that."

"A *Lady* Story! Oh, but that would be so dull, wouldn't it?" inquired No. 6. "You can't make anything funny out of them, surely! Surely they never do half such odd things as cooks, and boys in buttons!"

"The ladies themselves think not, of course," was Aunt Judy's reply.

"Well, but what do you think, Aunt Judy?"

"Oh, I don't think it matters what I think. The question is, what do cooks and boys in buttons think?"

"But, Aunt Judy, ladies are never tiresome, and idle, and impertinent, like cooks and boys in buttons. Oh! if you had but heard the *real* Cook Stories those ladies told! I say, let me tell you one or two - I do think I can remember them, if I try."

"Then don't try on any account, dear No. 6," exclaimed Aunt Judy. "I like make-believe Cook Stories much better than real ones."

"So do I!" cried No. 7, "they're so much the more entertaining."

"And not a bit less useful," subjoined Aunt Judy, with a sly smile.

"Well, I didn't see much good in the real ones," pursued No. 7, in a sort of muse.

"Let us tell you another make-believe one, then," cried No. 6, who saw that Aunt Judy was moving off, and wanted to detain her.

"Then it's *my* turn!" shouted No. 8, jumping up, and stretching out his arm and hand like a young orator flushed to his work. And actually, before the rest of the little ones could put him down or stop him, No. 8 contrived to tumble out the Cook Story idea, which had probably been brewing in his head all the time of Aunt Judy's talk.

It was very brief, and this was it, delivered in much haste, and with all the earnestness of a maiden speech.

"*I* had a button boy too, and he was a - what d'ye call it - oh, a *rascal,* that was it; - he was a rascal, and liked the currants in mince-pies, so he took them all out, and ate them up, and put in glass beads instead. So when the people began to ear, their teeth crunched against the beads! Ah! bah! how nasty it was!"

No. 8 accompanied this remark with a corresponding grimace of disgust, and then observed in conclusion:-

"Perhaps he found it in a book, but I don't know where," after which he lowered his outstretched arm, smiled, and sat down.

The company clapped applause, and No. 4 especially must have been very fond of laughing, for the glass-bead anecdote set her off again as heartily as ever, and the rest followed in her wake, and while so doing, never noticed that Aunt Judy had slipped away.

They soon discovered it, however, when their mirth

began to subside; but before they had time to wonder much, there appeared from behind the door of the wardrobe a figure, which in their secret souls they knew to be Aunt Judy herself, although it looked a great deal stouter, and had a thick-filled cap on its head, a white linen apron over its gown, and a pair of spectacles on its nose. At sight of it they showed signs of clapping again, but stopped short when it spoke to them as a stranger, and willingly received it as such.

Ah! it is one of the sweet features of childhood that it yields itself up so readily to any little surprise or delusion that is prepared for its amusement. No nasty pride, no disinclination to be carried away, no affected indifference, interfere with young children's enjoyment of what is offered them. They will even help themselves into the pleasant visions by an effort of will; and perhaps, now and then, end by partly believing what they at first received voluntarily as an agreeable make-believe.

If, therefore, after the cook figure of Aunt Judy had seated itself by the doll's table, and the little ones had looked and grinned at it for some time, hazy sensations began to steal over one or two minds, that this *was* somehow really a cook, it was all in the natural course of things, and nobody resisted the feeling.

Aunt Judy's altered voice, and odd, assumed manner, contributed, no doubt, a good deal to the impression.

"Dear, dear! what pretty little darlings you all are!" she began, looking at them one after another. "As sweet as sugar-plums, when you have your own way, and are pleased. Eh, dears? But you don't think you can take old Cooky in, do you? No, no, I know what ladies and gentlemen, and ladies' and gentlemen's *young* ladies and *young* gentlemen are, pretty well, dears, I can tell you! Don't I know all about the shiny hair and smiling faces of the little pets in the parlour, and how they leave parlour-manners behind them sometimes, when they run to the kitchen to Cook, and order her here and there, and want half-a-dozen things at once, and must and will have what they want, and are for popping their fingers into every pie!

"Well, well," she proceeded, "the parlour's the parlour, and the kitchen's the kitchen, and I'm only a cook. But then I conduct myself *as* Cook, even when I'm in the scullery, and I only wish ladies, and ladies' *young* ladies too, would conduct themselves as ladies, even when they come into the kitchen; that's what I call being honourable and upright. Well, dears, I'll tell you how I came to know all about it. You see, I lived once in a family where there were no less than eight of those precious little pets, and a precious time I had of it with them. But, to be sure, now it's past and gone - I can make plenty of excuses for them, poor things! They were so coaxed and flattered, and made so much of, what could be expected from them but tiresome, wilful ways, without any sense?

"'If your mamma would but put *you* into the scullery, young miss, to learn to wash plates and scour the pans out, she'd make a woman of you,' used I to think to myself when a silly child, who thought itself very clever to hinder other people's work, would come hanging about in the kitchen, doing nothing but teaze and find fault, for that's what a girl can always do.

"It was very aggravating, you may be sure, dears, (you see I can talk to you quite reasonably, because you're so nicely behaved;) - it was very aggravating, of course; but I used to make allowances for them. Says I to myself, 'Cook, you've had the blessing of being brought up to hard work ever since you were a babby. You've had to earn your daily bread. Nobody knows how that brings people to their senses till they've tried; so don't you go and be cocky, because ladies and gentlemen, and ladies' and gentlemen's *young* ladies and *young* gentlemen, are not quite so sensible as you are. Who knows but what, if you'd been born to do nothing, you might have been no wiser than them! It's lucky for you you're only a cook; but don't you go and be cocky, that's all! Make allowances; it's the secret of life!'

"So you see, dears, I *did* make allowances; and after the eight little pets was safe in bed till next morning, I used to feel quite composed, and pitiful-like towards them, poor little dears! But certainly, when morning came, and the oldest young master was home for the holidays, it was a trying time for me, and I couldn't think of the allowances any longer. Either he wouldn't get up and come down till everyone else had had their breakfast, and so he wanted fresh water boiled, and fresh tea made, and another muffin toasted, and more bacon fried; or else he was up so outrageous early, that he was scolding because there was no hot water before the fire was lit - bless you, he hadn't a bit of sense in his head, poor boy, not a bit! And how should he? Why, he went to school as soon as he was out of petticoats, and was set to all that Latin and Greek stuff that never puts anything useful into folks' heads, but so much more chatter and talk; so he came back as silly as he went, poor thing! Dear me, on a wet day, after lesson-time, those boys were like so many crazy creatures. 'Cook, I must make a pie,' says one.

Mrs Alfred Gatty

'There's a pie in the oven already, Master James,' says I. 'I don't care about the pie in the oven,' says he, 'I want a pie of my own. Bring me the flour, and the water, and the butter, and all the things - and, above all, the rolling-pin - and clear the decks, will you, I say, for my pie. Here goes!' And here used to go, my dears, for Master James had no sense, as I told you; and so he'd shove all my pots and dishes away, one on the top of the other; and let me be as busy as I would, and dinner ever so near ready, the dresser must be cleared, and everything must give way to *his* pie! His pie, indeed - I wish I had had the management of his pie just then! I'd have taught him what it was to come shaking the rolling-pin at the head of a respectable cook, who wanted to get her business done properly, as in duty bound!

"But he wasn't the only one. There was little Whipper-snapper, his younger brother, squeaking out in another corner, 'I shan't make a pie, James, I shall make toffey; it's far better fun. You'd better come and help me. Where's the treacle pot, Cook? Cook! I say, Cook! where's the treacle-pot? And look at this stupid kettle and pan. What's in the pan, I wonder? Oh, kidney-beans! Who cares for kidney-beans? How can I make toffey, when all these things are on the fire? Stay, I'll hand them all off!'

"And, sure enough, if I hadn't rushed from Master James, who was drinking away at my custard out of the bowl, to seize on Whipper-snapper, who had got his hand on the vegetable-pan already, he would have pulled it and the kettle, and the whole concern, off the fire, and perhaps scalded himself to death.

"Then, of course, there comes a scuffle, and Master

Whipper-snapper begins to roar, and out comes Missus, who, poor thing, had no more sense in her head than her sons, though she'd never been to school to lose it over Latin and Greek; and, says she, with all her ribbons streaming, and her petticoats swelled out like a window-curtain in a draught - says she:-

"'Cook! I desire that you will not touch my children!'

"'As you please, ma'am,' says I, 'if you'll be so good as to stop the young gentlemen from touching my pans, and - ' I was going to say 'custard,' but Master James shouts out quite quick:-

"'Why, I only wanted to make a pie, mamma.'

"'And I only wanted to make some toffey!' cries Whipper-snapper; and then mamma answers, like a duchess at court:-

"'There can't possibly be any objection, my dears; and I wish, Cook, you would he a little more good-natured to the children; - your temper is sadly against you!'

"And out she sails, ribbons and window-curtains and all; and, says I to myself, as I cooled down, (for the young gentlemen luckily went away with their dear mama,) - says I to myself, 'It's a very fine thing, no doubt, to go about in ribbons, and petticoats, and grand clothes; but, if one must needs carry such a poor, silly head inside them, as Missus does, I'd rather stop as I am, and be a cook with some sense about me.'

"I don't say, my dears," continued the supposed cook, "that I spoke very politely just then; but who could feel polite, when their dinner had been put back at least half-an-hour over such nonsense as that? Missus used to say the 'dear boys' came to the kitchen on a wet day, because they'd got *nothing else to do*! Nothing else to do! and had learnt Latin and Greek, and all sorts of schooling besides! So much for education, thought I. Why, it would spoil the best lads that ever were born into the world. For, of course, you know if these young gentlemen had been put to decent trades, they'd have found something else to do with their fingers besides mischief and waste. And, dear me, I talk about not having been polite to Missus just then, but now you tell me, dears, what Missus, with all her education, would have said if she'd been in my place, when one young gentleman was drinking her custard, and another young gentleman was pulling her pans on the floor! Do you think she'd have been a bit more polite than I was? Wouldn't she have called me all the stupid creatures that ever were born, and told the story over and over to all her friends and acquaintance to make them stare, and say there were surely no such simpletons in the world as ladies and gentlemen, and ladies' and gentlemen's young ladies and young gentlemen?

"However, I did not go as far as that, because, you see, I had some sense about me, and could make allowances for all the nonsense the poor things are brought up to."

There was no resisting the twinkle in Aunt Judy's eye when she came to this point, though it shone through an old pair of Nurse's spectacles; and the little ones clapped their hands, and declared it was every bit as good as a Cook story, *only a great deal better*! That twinkle had quite brought Aunt Judy back to them again, in spite of her cook's attire, and No. 6

cried out:-

"Oh! don't stop, Aunt Judy! Do go on, Cooky dear! do tell some more! Did you always live in that place, please?"

"There now!" exclaimed Aunt Judy, throwing herself back in the chair, "isn't that a regular young lady's question, out and out? Who but a young lady, with no more sense in her head than a pin, would have thoughtof asking such a thing? Why, miss, is there a joint in the world that can bear basting for ever? No, no! a time comes when it must be taken down, if any good's to be left in it; and so at the end of three years my basting-time was over, and the time for taking down was come.

"'Cook,' says I to myself, 'you must give in. If you go on with those cherubs (that was their company name, you know) much longer, there won't be a bit of you left!' And, sure enough, that very morning, dears, they'd come down upon me with a fresh grievance, and I couldn't stand it, I really couldn't! The sweeps had been by four o'clock to the kitchen chimney, and I'd been up and toiling every minute since, and hadn't had time to eat my breakfast, when in they burst - the young ladies, not the sweeps, dears, I mean:- and there they broke out at once - I hadn't fed their sea-gulls before breakfast - (a couple of dull-looking grey birds, with big mouths, that had come in a hamper over night as a present to the cherubs;) and it seems I ought to have been up before daylight almost, to look for slugs for them in the garden till they'd got used to the place!

"Oh, these ladies and gentlemen! they'd need know something of some sort to make amends, for there are many things they never know all their life long!

"'Young ladies,' says I, 'I didn't come here to get meals ready for sea-gulls, but Christian ladies and gentlemen. If the sea-gulls want a cook, your mamma must hire them one on purpose. I've plenty to do for her and the family, without looking after such nonsense as that!'

"'That's what you always say,' whimpers the youngest Miss; 'and you know they don't want any cooking, but only raw slugs! And you know you might easily look for them, because you've got almost nothing to do, because it's such an easy place, mamma always says. But you're always cross, mamma says that too, and everybody knows you are, because she tells everybody!'

"When little Miss had got that out, she thought she'd finished me up; and so she had, for when I heard that Missus was so ungenteel as to go talking of what I did, to all her acquaintance, and had nothing better to talk about, I made up my mind that I'd give notice that very day.

"'Very well, miss,' says I, 'your mamma shall soon have something fresh to talk about, and I hope she'll find it a pleasant change.'

"There was some of them knew what I meant at once, for after they'd scampered off I heard shouts up and down the stairs from one to the other, 'Cook's going!' 'We shall have a new cook soon!' 'What a lark we'll have with the toffey and the pies! We'll make her do just as we choose!'

"'There, now,' thought I to myself, 'there'll be somebody else put down to baste before long. Well, I'm glad my time's over.' And thereupon I fell to wishing I was back again in father and mother's ricketty old cottage, that I'd once been so proud to leave, to go and live with gentlefolks. But, you see, it was no use wishing, for I'd my bread to earn, and must turn out somewhere, let it be as disagreeable as it would. Father and mother were dead, and there was no ricketty cottage for me to go back to, so I wiped my eyes, and told myself to make the best of what had to be.

"Well, dears," pursued Cooky, after a short pause, during which the little ones looked far more inclined to cry than laugh, "Missus was quite taken aback when she heard I wouldn't stay any longer.

"'Cook,' she said, 'I'm perfectly astonished at your want of sense in not recognizing the value of such a situation as mine! and as to your complaints about the children, anything more ridiculously unreasonable I never heard! Such superior, well-taught young people, you are not very likely to meet with again in a hurry!'

"'Perhaps not, ma'am,' says I, 'in French, and crochet, and the piano, and Latin, and things I don't understand, being only a cook. But I know what behaviour is, and that's what I'm sure the young ladies and gentlemen have never been taught; or if they have, they're so slow at taking it in, that I think I shall do better with a family where the behaviour-lessons come first!'

"Missus was very angry, and so was I; but at last she said:-

"'Cook, I shall not argue with you any longer; you know no better, and I suppose I must make allowances for you.'

"'I'm much obliged to you, ma'am, I'm sure,' was my answer; 'it's what I've always done by you ever since I came to the house, and I'll do it still with pleasure, and think no more of what's been said.'

"I spoke from my heart, I can tell you, dears, for I felt very sorry for Missus, and thought she was but a lady after all, and perhaps I'd hardly made allowances enough. I'd lost my temper, too, as I knew after she went away. But, you see, while she was there, it was so mortifying to be spoken to as if all the sense was on her side, when I knew it was all on mine, wherever the French and crochet may have been. Well, but the day before I left, I broke down with another of them, as it's fair that you should know.

"I'd felt very lonely that day, busy as I was, and in the afternoon I took myself into the scullery to give the pans a sort of good-bye cleaning, and be out of every-body's way. But there, in the midst of it, comes the eldest young gentleman flinging into the kitchen, shouting, 'Cook! Cook! Where's Cook?' as usual. I thought he was after some of his old tricks, and I *had* been fretting over those pans, thinking what a sad job it was to have no home to go to in the world, so I gave him a very short answer.

"'Master James,' says I, 'I've done with nonsense now, I can't attend to you. You must wait till the next cook comes.'

"But Master James came straight away to the scullery

door, and says he, 'Cook, I'm not coming to teaze. I've brought you a needle-book. There, Cook! It's full of needles. I put them all in myself. Keep it, please.'

"Dear, dear, I can't forget it yet," pursued Cook, "how Master James stood on the little stone step of the scullery, with his arm stretched out, and the needle-book that he'd bought for me in his hand. I don't know how I thanked him, I'm sure; but I had to go back to the sink and wash the dirt off my hands before I could touch the pretty little thing, and then I told him I would keep it as long as ever I lived.

"He laughed, and says he, 'Now shake hands, Cooky,' and so we shook hands; and then off he ran, and I went back to my pans and fairly cried.

"'Why, Cook,' says I to myself, 'that lad's got as good a heart as your own, after all. And as to sense and behaviour, they haven't been forced upon him yet, as they have upon you. Latin's Latin, and conduct's conduct, and one doesn't teach the other; and it's too bad to expect more of people than what they've had opportunity for.'

Well, dears, that was the rule I always went by, and I've been in many situations since - with single ladies, and single gentlemen, and large families, and all; and there was something to put up with in all of them; and they always told me there was a good deal to put up with in me, and perhaps there was. However, it doesn't matter, so long as Missus and servant go by one rule - *to make allowances, and not expect more from people than what they've had opportunity for;* and, above all, never to be cocky when all the advantage is on their own side. It's a good rule, dears, and will stop many a foolish word and idle tale, if you'll go by it."

Aunt Judy had finished at last, and she took off the old spectacles and laid them on the doll's table, and paused.

"It *is* a good rule," observed No. 4, "and I shall go by it, and not tell real Cook Stories when I grow up, I hope."

"I love old Cooky," cried No. 6, getting up and hugging her round the neck; "but is it wrong, Aunt Judy, to tell funny make-believe Cook Stories, like ours?"

"Not at all, No. 6," replied Aunt Judy. "My private belief is, that if you tell funny make-believe Cook Stories while you're little, you will be ashamed of telling stupid real ones when you're grown up."

RABBITS' TAILS.

"Death and its two-fold aspect! wintry - one,
Cold, sullen, blank, from hope and joy shut out;
The other, which the ray divine hath touch'd,
Replete with vivid promise, bright as spring."
WORDSWORTH.

"Well then; but you must remember that I have been ill, and cannot be expected to invent anything very entertaining."

"Oh, we do remember, indeed, Aunt Judy; we have been so miserable," was the answer; and the speaker added, shoving her little chair close up to her sister's:-

"I said if you were not to get better, I shouldn't want to get better either."

"Hush, hush, No. 6!" exclaimed Aunt Judy, quite startled by the expression; "it was not right to say or think that."

"I couldn't help it," persisted No. 6. "We couldn't do without you, I'm sure."

"We can do without anything which God chooses to take away," was Aunt Judy's very serious answer.

Mrs Alfred Gatty

"But I didn't want to do without," murmured No. 6, with her eyes fixed on the floor.

"Dear No. 6, I know," replied Aunt Judy, kindly; "but that is just what you must try not to feel."

"I can't help feeling it," reiterated No. 6, still looking down.

"You have not tried, or thought about it yet," suggested her sister; "but do think. Think what poor ignorant infants we all are in the hands of God, not knowing what is either good or bad for us; and then you will see how glad and thankful you ought to be, to be chosen for by somebody wiser than yourself. We must always be contented with God's choice about whatever happens."

No. 6 still looked down, as if she were studying the pattern of the rug, but she saw nothing of it, for her eyes were swimming over with the tears that had filled into them, and at last she said:-

"I could, perhaps, about some things, but *only not that* about you. Aunt Judy, you know what I mean."

Aunt Judy leant back in her chair. *"Only not that."* It was, as she knew, the cry of the universal world, although it broke now from the lips of a child. And it was painful, though touching, to feel herself the treasure that could not be parted with.

So there was a silence of some minutes, during which the hand of the little sister lay in that of the elder one.

But the latter soon roused up and spoke.

"I'll tell you what, No. 6, there's nothing so foolish as talking of how we shall feel, and what we shall do, if so-and-so happens. Perhaps it never may happen, or, if it does, perhaps we may be helped to bear it quite differently from what we have expected. So we won't say anything more about it now."

"I'm so glad!" exclaimed No. 6, completely reassured and made comfortable by the cheerful tone of her sister's remark, though she had but a very imperfect idea of the meaning of it, as she forthwith proved by rambling off into a sort of self-defence and self-justification.

"And I'm not really a baby now, you know, Aunt Judy! And I do know a great many things that are good and bad for us. I know that *you* are good for us, even when you scold over sums."

"That is a grand admission, I must own," replied Aunt Judy, smiling; "I shall remind you of it some day."

"Well, you may," cried No. 6, earnestly; and added, "you see I'm not half as silly as you thought."

Aunt Judy looked at her, wondering how she should get the child to understand what was passing through her own mind; wondering, too whether it was right to make the attempt; and she decided that on the whole it was; so she answered:-

"Ay, we grow wise enough among ourselves as we grow older, and get to know a few more things. You are certainly a little wiser than a baby in long petticoats, and I am a little wiser than you, and mamma wiser than us both. But towards God we remain ignorant infants all our lives. That was what I meant."

"But surely, Aunt Judy," interrupted No. 6, "mamma and you know - " There she stopped.

"Nothing about God's dealings," pursued Aunt Judy, "but that they are sure to be good for us, even when we like them least, and cannot understand them at all. We know so little what we ought really to like and dislike, dear No. 6, that we often fret and cry as foolishly as the two children did, who, while they were in mourning for their mother, broke their hearts over the loss of a set of rabbits' tails."

No. 6 sprang up at the idea. She had never heard of those children before. Who were they? Had Aunt Judy read of them in a book, or were they real children? How could they have broken their hearts about rabbits' tails? It must be a very curious story, and No. 6 begged to hear it.

Aunt Judy had, however, a little hesitation about the matter. There was something sad about the story; and there was no exact teaching to be got out of it, though certainly if it helped to shake No. 6's faith in her own wisdom, a good effect would be produced by listening to it. Also it was not a bad thing now and then to hear of other people having to bear trials which have not fallen to our own lot. It must surely have a tendency to soften the heart, and make us feel more dependent upon the God who gives and takes away. On the whole, therefore, she would tell the story, so she made No. 6 sit quietly down again, and began as follows:-

"There were once upon a time two little motherless girls."

No. 6's excitement of expectation was hardly over, so she tightened her hand over Aunt Judy's, and ejaculated:-

"Poor little things!"

"You may well say so," continued Aunt Judy. "It was just what everybody said who saw them at the time. When they went about with their widowed father in the country village where 'they lived, even the poor women who stood at their cottage door-steads, would look after them when they had passed, and say with a sigh:-

"'Poor little things!'

"When they went up to London in the winter to stay with their grandmamma, and walked about in the Square in their little black frocks and crape-trimmed bonnets, the ladies who saw them, - even comparative strangers, - would turn round arid say:-

"'Poor little things!'

"If visitors came to call at the house, and the children were sent for into the room, there was sure to be a whispered exclamation directly among the grown-up people of, 'Poor little things!' But oh, No. 6! the children themselves did not think about it at all. What did they know, - poor little things, - of the real misfortune which had befallen them! They were sorry, of course, at first, when they did not see their mamma as usual, and when she did not come back to them as

Mrs Alfred Gatty

soon as they expected. But some separation had taken place during her illness; and sometimes before, she had been poorly and got well again; and sometimes she had gone out visiting, and they had had to do without her till she returned; and so, although the days and weeks of her absence went on to months, still it was only the same thing they had felt before, continued rather longer; and meantime the little events of each day rose up to distract their attention. They got up, and dined, and went to bed as usual. They were sometimes merry, sometimes naughty, as usual. People made them nice presents, or sent for them to pleasant treats, as usual - perhaps more than usual; their father did all he could to supply the place of the lost one, but never could name her name; and soon they forgot that they had ever had a mamma at all. Soon? Ay, long before friends and strangers lead left off saying 'Poor little things' at sight of them, and long before the black frocks and crape-trimmed bonnets were laid aside, which, indeed, they wore double the usual length of time."

"And how old were they?" asked No. 6, in a whisper.

"Four and five," replied Aunt Judy; "old enough to know what they liked and disliked from hour to hour. Old enough to miss what had pleased them, till something else pleased them as well. But not old enough to look forward and know how much a mother is wanted in life; and, therefore, what a terrible loss the loss of a mother is."

"It's a very sad story I'm afraid," remarked No. 6.

"Not altogether," said Aunt Judy, smiling, "as you shall hear. One day the two little motherless girls went hand in hand across one of the courts of the great

Charity Institution in London, where their grand-mamma lived, into the old archway entrance, and there they stood still, looking round them, as if waiting for something. The old archway entrance opened into a square, and underneath its shelter there was a bench on one side, and on the other the lodge of the porter, whose business it was to shut up the great gates at night.

The porter had often before looked at the motherless children as they passed into the shadow of his archway, and said to himself, 'Poor little things;' for just so, during many years of his life, he had watched their young mother pass through, and had exchanged words of friendly greeting with her.

"And even now, although it was at least a year and a half since her death, when he saw the waiting children seat themselves on the bench opposite his door, the old thought stole over his mind. How sad that she should have been taken away so early from those little ones! How sad for them to be left! No one - nothing - in this world, could supply the loss of her protecting care. - *Poor little things*! - and not the less so because they were altogether unconscious of their misfortune; and here, with the mourning casting a gloom over their fair young faces, were looking with the utmost eagerness and delight towards the doorway, - now and then slipping down from their seats to take a peep into the Square, and see if what they expected was coming, - now and then giggling to each other about the grave face of the old man on the other side of the way.

"At last, one, who had been peeping a bit as before, exclaimed, with a smothered shout, 'Here he is!' and then the other joined her, and the two rushed out together into the Square and stood on the pavement, stopping the way in front of a lad, who held over his arm a basket containing hares' and rabbits' skins, in which he carried on a small trade.

"They looked up with their smiling faces into his, and he grinned at them in return, and then they said, 'Have you got any for us to-day?' on which he set down his basket before them, and told them they might have one or two if they pleased, and down they knelt upon the pavement, examining the contents of his basket, and talked in almost breathless whispers to each other of the respective merits, the softness, colour, and prettiness, of - what do you think?"

At the first moment No. 6, being engrossed by the story, could not guess at all; but in another instant she recollected, and exclaimed:-

"Oh, Aunt Judy, do you mean those were the rabbits' tails you told about?"

"They were indeed, No. 6," replied Aunt Judy; "their grandmamma's cook had given them one or two sometime before, and there being but few entertaining games which two children can play at alone, and these poor little things being a good deal left to themselves, they invented a play of their own out of the rabbits' tails. I think the pleasant feel of the fur, which was so nice to cuddle and kiss, helped them to this odd liking; but whatever may have been the cause, certain it is they did get quite fond of them - pretended that they could feel, and were real living things, and talked of them, and to them, as if they were a party of children.

"They called them 'Tods' and 'Toddies,' but they had

all sorts of names besides, to distinguish one from the other. There was, 'Whity,' and 'Browny,' and 'Softy,' and 'Snuggy,' and 'Stripy,' and many others. They knew almost every hair of each of them, and I believe could have told which was which, in the dark, merely by their feel.

"This sounds ridiculous enough, does it not, dear No. 6?" said Aunt Judy, interrupting herself.

No. 6 smiled, but she was too much interested to wish to talk; so the story proceeded.

"Now you must know that I have looked rather curiously at hares' and rabbits' tails myself since I first heard the story; and there actually is more variety in them than you would suppose. Some are nice little fat things - almost round, with the hair close and fine; others longer and more skinny, and with poor hair, although what there is may be of a handsome colour. And as to colour, even in rabbits' tails, which are white underneath, there are all shades from grey to dark brown one the upper side; and the patterns and markings differ, as you know they do on the fur of a cat. In short, there really is a choice even in hares' and rabbits' tails, and the more you look at them, the more delicate distinctions you will see.

"Well, the poor little girls knew all about this, and a great deal more, I dare say, than I have noticed, for they had played at fancy-life with them, till the Tods had become far more to them than any toys they possessed; actually, in fact, things to love; and I dare say if we could have watched them at night putting their Tods to bed, we should have seen every one of them kissed.

Mrs Alfred Gatty

"It was a capital thing, as you may suppose, for keeping the children quiet as well as happy in the nursery, at the top of the London house, in one particular corner of which the basket of Tods was kept. But when grandmamma's bell rang, which it did day by day as a summons, after the parlour breakfast was over, the Tods were put away; and it was dolls, or reasonable toys of some description, which the motherless little girls took down with them to the drawing-room; and I doubt whether either grand-mamma or aunt knew of the Tod family in the basket up-stairs.

"After the affair had gone on for a little time, the children were accidentally in the kitchen when the rabbit-skin dealer called, and the cook begged him to give them a tail or two; and thenceforth, of course, they looked upon him as one of their greatest friends; and if they wanted fresh Tods, they would lie in wait for him in the archway entrance, for fear he should go by without coming in to call at their grandmamma's house. And on the day I have described, two new brothers, 'Furry' and 'Buffy,' were introduced to the Tod establishment, and the talking and delight that ensued, lasted for the whole afternoon.

"Nobody knew, I believe; but certainly if anybody had known how the hearts of those children were getting involved over the dead rabbits' tails, it would have been only right to have tried to lead their affection into some better direction. What a waste of good emotions it was, when they cuddled up their Tods in an evening; invented histories of what they had said and done during the day, and put them by at last with caresses something very nearly akin to human love!"

"Oh, dear Aunt Judy," exclaimed No. 6, "if their poor mamma had but been there!"

"All would have been right then, would it not, No. 6?"

No. 6 said "Yes" from the very depths of her heart.

"*As it seems to us,* you should say," continued Aunt Judy; "but that is all. It could not have seemed so to the God who took their mother away."

"Aunt Judy - "

"No. 6, I am telling you a very serious truth. Had it indeed been right for the children that their mother should have lived, she would *not* have been taken away. For some reason or other it was necessary that they should be without the comfort, and help, and protection, of her presence in this world. We cannot understand it, but a time may come when we may see it all as clearly as we now see the folly of those children who so doted upon senseless rabbits' tails."

"Oh, Aunt Judy, but it was still very, very sad."

"Yes, about that there cannot be a doubt, and I am as much inclined as anybody else to say, 'Poor little things' every time I mention them. But now let me go on with the story, for it has a sort of end as well as beginning. The Tod affair came at last to their grandmamma's ears."

"I am so glad," cried No. 6.
"You will not say so when I tell you how it happened," was Aunt Judy's rejoinder. "The fact was, that one unfortunate day one of the Tods disappeared. Whether

it lead been left out of the basket when grandmamma's bell rang, and so got swept away by the nurse and burnt, I cannot say; but, at any rate, when the children went to their play one morning, 'Softy,' their dear little 'Softy,' was gone. He was the fattest-furred and finest-haired of all the Tod family, and the one about whom they invented the prettiest stories; he was, in fact, the model, the out-of-the-way-amiable pattern Tod. They could not believe at first that he really was gone. They hunted for him in every hole and corner of their nursery and bed-room; they looked for him all along the passages; they tossed all the other Tods out of the basket to find him, as if they really were - even in their eyes - nothing but rabbits' tails; they asked all the servants about him, till everybody's patience was exhausted, and they got angry; and then at last the children's hope and temper were both exhausted too, and they broke out into passionate crying.

"This was vexatious to the nurse, of course; but her method of consolation was not very judicious.

"'Why, bless my heart,' was her beginning, 'what nonsense! Didn't the children know as well as she did, that hares' and rabbits' tails were not alive, and couldn't feel? and what could it signify of one of them was thrown away and lost? They'd a basket-full left besides, and it was plenty of such rubbish as that! They were all very well to play with up in the nursery, but they were worth nothing when all was said and done!'

This was completely in vain, of course. The children sat on the nursery floor and cried on just the same; and by-and-by went away to the corner of the room where the Tod-basket was kept, and bewailed the loss of poor

'Softy' to his brothers and sisters inside.

"As the time approached, however, for grandmamma's summoning bell, the nurse began to wonder what she could do to stop this fretting, and cool the red eyes; so she tried the coaxing plan, by way of a change.

"'If she was such nice little girls with beautiful dolls and toys, she never would fret so about a rabbit's tail, to be sure! And, besides, the boy was sure to be round again very soon with the hare and rabbit skins; and if they would only be good, and dry their eyes, she would get him to give them as many more as they pleased. Quite fresh new ones. She dared say they would be as pretty again as the one that was lost.'

"If nurse had wished to hit upon an injudicious remark, she could not have succeeded better. What did they care for 'fresh new' Tods instead of their dear 'Softy?' And the mere suggestion that any others could be prettier, turned their regretful love into a sort of passionate indignation; yet the nurse had meant well, and was astonished when the conclusion of what was intended to be a kind harangue, was followed by a louder burst of crying than ever.

"It must be owned that the little girls had by this time got out of grief into naughtiness; and there was now quite as much petted temper as sorrow in their tears; and lo! while they were in the midst of this fretful condition, grandmamma's summoning bell was heard, and they were obliged to go down to her.

"You can just imagine their appearance when they entered the drawing-room with their eyes red and swelled, their cheeks flushed, and anything but a pleasant expression over their faces. Of course, grand-mamma and aunt immediately made inquiries as to the reason of so much disturbance, but the children were scarcely able to utter the usual 'good morning;' and when called upon to tell their cause of trouble, did nothing but begin to cry afresh.

"Whereupon their aunt was dispatched up-stairs to find out what was amiss; and then, for the first time, she heard from the nurse the history of the Tod family, the children's devotion to them, and their present vexatious grief about the loss of a solitary one of what she called their stupid bits of nonsense.

"Foolish as the whole affair sounds in looking back upon it, it certainly was one which required rather delicate handling, and I doubt whether anybody but a mother could have handled it properly. Grandmamma and aunt had every wish to do for the best, but they hardly took enough into consideration, either the bereaved condition of those motherless little ones, or their highly fanciful turn of mind. Yet nobody was to blame; the children spent all the summer with their father in the country, and all the winter with their grandmamma in London; and, therefore, no continued knowledge of their characters was possible, for they were always birds of passage everywhere. Certainly, however, it was a great mistake, under such circum-stances, for grandmamma and aunt to have broken rudely into the one stronghold of childish comfort, which they had raised up for themselves."

Aunt Judy paused, and No. 6 really looked frightened as to what was coming next, and asked what Aunt Judy could mean that they did. "Were they very angry?" "No, they were not very angry," Aunt Judy said;

"perhaps if they had been only that, the whole thing would have passed over and been forgotten.

"But they held grave consultation upon the subject, and made it too serious, in my opinion, and I dare say you will think so too. Meantime the naughty children were turned out of the room while they talked, and the mystery of this, sobered their temper considerably; so that they made no further disturbance, but wandered up and down the stairs, and about the hall, in silent discomfort.

"At one time they thought they heard the drawing-room door open, and their aunt go up-stairs towards the nursery department again; but then for a long while they heard no more; and at last, childlike, began to amuse themselves by seeing how far along the oil-cloth pattern they could each step, as they walked the length of the hall, the great object being to stretch from one particular diamond to another, without touching any intermediate mark.

"In the midst of the excitement of this, they heard their aunt's voice calling to them from the middle of the last flight of stairs. There was something in her face, composed as it was, which alarmed them directly, and there they stood quite still, gazing at her.

"'Grandmamma and I,' she began, 'think you have been very silly indeed in making such a fuss about those rabbits' tails; and you have been very naughty indeed to-day, *very naughty,* in crying so ridiculously, and teazing all the servants, because of one being lost. You can't play with them rationally, nurse is sure, and so we think you will be very much better without them. Grandmamma has sent me to tell you - *You will never see the Tods, as you call them, any more.'*

"Aunt Judy, it was horrible!" cried No. 6; "savage and horrible!" she repeated, and burst the next instant into a flood of tears.

"Oh, my old darling No. 6," cried Aunt Judy, covering the sobbing child quite round with both her arms, "surely *you* are not going into hysterics about the rabbits' tails too! I doubt if even their little mammas did that. Come! you must cheer up, or mamma will leave to be sent for to say that if you are so unreasonable, you must never listen to Aunt Judy's stories any more."

No. 6's emotion began to subside under the comfortable embrace, and Aunt Judy's joke provoked a smile.

"There now, that's good!" cried Aunt Judy; "and now, if you won't be ridiculous, I will finish the story. I almost think the prettiest part is to come."

This was consolation indeed; but No. 6 could not resist a remark.

"But, Aunt Judy, wasn't that aunt - "

"Hush, hush," interrupted Aunt Judy, "I apologized for both aunt and grandmamma before I told you what they did. They meant to do for the best, and

'The best can do no more.'

They cured the evil too, though in what you and I think rather a rough manner. And rough treatment is some-times very effectual, however unpleasant. It was but a preparation for the much harder disappointments of older life."

"Poor little things!" ejaculated No. 6, once more. "Just tell me if they cried dreadfully."

"I don't think I care to talk much about that, dear No. 6," answered her sister. "They had cried almost as much as they could do in one day, and were stupified by the new misfortune, besides which, they had a feeling all the time of having brought it on themselves by being dreadfully naughty. It was a sad muddle altogether, I must confess. The shock upon the poor children's minds at the time must have been very great, for the memory of that bereavement clung to them through grown-up life, as a very unpleasant recollection, when a thousand more important things had passed away forgotten from their thoughts. In fact, as I said, the motherless little girls really broke their hearts over a parcel of rabbits' tails. But I must go on with the story. After a day or two of dull desolation, the children wearied even of their grief. And both grandmamma and aunt became very sorry for them, although the fatal subject of the Tods was never mentioned; but they bought them several beautiful toys which no child could help looking at or being pleased with. Among these presents was a brown fur dog, with a very nice face and a pair of bright black eyes, and a curly tail hung over his back in a particularly graceful manner; and this was, as you may suppose, in the children's eyes, the gem of all their new treasures. The feel of him reminded them of the lost Tods; and in every respect he was, of course, superior. They named him 'Carlo,' and in a quiet manner established him as the favourite creature of their play. And thus, by degrees, and as time went on, their grief for the loss of the Tods abated somewhat; and at last they began to talk about them to each other, which was a sure sign that their feelings were softened.

"But you will never guess what turn their conversation took. They did not begin to say how sorry they had been, or were; nor did they make any angry remarks about their aunt's cruelty; but one day as they were sitting playing with Carlo, in what may be called the Tod corner of the nursery, the eldest child said suddenly to her sister, in a low voice

"'What do you think our aunt has *really* done with the Tods?'

"A question which seemed not at all to surprise the other, for she answered, in the same mysterious tone:-

"'I don't know, but I don't think she *could* burn them.'

"'And I don't, either,' was the rejoinder. 'Perhaps she has only put them somewhere where *we* cannot get at them.'

"The next idea came from the younger child:-

"'Do you think she'll ever let us have them back again?'

"But the answer to this was a long shake of the head from the wiser elder sister. And then they began to play with Carlo again.

"But after that day they used often to exchange a few words together on the subject, although only to the same effect - their aunt *could* not have burnt them, they felt sure. She never said she had burnt them. She only said, '*You will never see the Tods any more.*'

"Perhaps she had only put them by; perhaps she had put them by in some comfortable place; perhaps they were in their little basket in some closet, or corner of the house, quite as snug as up in the nursery.

"And here the conversation would break off again. As to asking any questions of their aunt, *that* was a thing that never crossed their minds. It was impossible; the subject was so fatally serious! . . . But I believe there was an involuntary peeping about into closets and out-of-the-way places whenever opportunity offered; yet no result followed, and the Tods were not found.

"One night, two or three months later, and just before the little things were moved back from London to their country home; and when they were in bed in their sleeping room, as usual, and the nurse had left them, and had shut the door between them and the day nursery, where she sat at work, the elder child called out in a whisper to the younger one:-

"'Sister, are you asleep?'

"'No. Why?'

"'I'll tell you of a place where the Tods may be.'

"'Where?'

"'The cellar.'

"'Do you think so?'

Mrs Alfred Gatty

"'Yes. I think we've looked everywhere else. And I think perhaps it's very nice down there with bits of sawdust here and there on the ground. I saw some on the bottle to-day, and it was quite soft. Aunt would be quite sure we should never see them there. I dare say it's very snug indeed all among the barrels and empty bottles in that cellar we once peeped into.'

"The younger child here began to laugh in delighted amusement, but the elder one bade her 'hush,' or the nurse would hear them; and then proceeded whispering as before

"'It's a great big place, and they could each have a house, and visit each other, and hide, and make fun.'

"'And I dare say Softy was put there first,' interposed the younger sister.

"'Ay, and how pleased the others would be to find him there! Only think!'

"And they *did* think. Poor little things, they lay and thought of that meeting when 'the others' were put in the cellar where 'Softy' already was, ready to welcome them to his new home; and they talked of all that might have happened on such an occasion, and told each other that the Tods were much happier altogether there, than if the others had remained in the nursery separated from dear little Softy. In short, they talked till the door opened, and the nurse, unsuspicious of the state of her young charges, went to bed herself, and sleep fell on the whole party.

"But a new world had now opened before them out of the very midst of their sorrow itself. The fancy home of the Tods was almost a more available source of amusement, than even playing with the real things had been; and sometimes in the early morning, sometimes for the precious half-hour at night, before sleep overtook them, the little wits went to work with fresh details and suppositions, and they related to each other, in turns, the imaginary events of the day in the cellar among the barrels. Each morning, when they went down-stairs, Carlo was put in the Tod corner of the nursery and instructed to slip away, as soon as he could manage it, to the Tods in the cellar, and hear all that they had been about.

"And marvellous tales Mr. Carlo used to bring back, if the children's accounts to each other were to be trusted. Such running about, to be sure, took place among those barrels and empty bottles. Such playing at bo-peep. Such visits of 'Furry' and his family to 'Buffy' and *his* family, when the little 'Furrys' and 'Buffys' could not be kept in order, but would go peeping into bungholes, and tumbling nearly through, and having to be picked out by Carlo, drabbled and chilled, but ready for a fresh frolic five minutes after!

"Such comical disputes, too, they had, as to how far the grounds round each Tod's house extended; such funny adventures of getting into their neighbour's corner instead of their own, in the dim light that prevailed, and being mistaken for a thief; when Carlo had to come and act as judge among them, and make them kiss and be friends all round!

"Such dinners, too, Carlo brought them, as he passed through the kitchen on his road to the cellar, and watched his opportunity to carry off a few un-missed little bits for his friends below. Dear me! his contrivances on that score were endless, and the odd things he got hold of sometimes by mistake, in his hurry, were enough to kill the Tods with laughing - to say nothing of the children who were inventing the history!

"Then the care they took to save the little drops at the bottom of the bottles, for Carlo, in return for all the trouble he had, was most praiseworthy; and sometimes, when there was a rather larger quantity than usual, they would have *such* a feast! - and drink the healths of their dear little mistresses in the nursery up-stairs.

"In short, it was as perfect a fancy as their love for the Tods, and their ideas of enjoyment could make it. Nothing uncomfortable, nothing sad, was ever heard of in that cellar-home of their lost pets. No quarrelling, no crying, no naughtiness, no unkindness, were supposed to trouble it. Nothing was known of, there, but comfort and fun, and innocent blunders and jokes, which ended in fun and comfort again. One thing, therefore, you see, was established as certain throughout the whole of the childish dream:- the departed favourites were all perfectly happy, as happy as it was possible to be; and they sent loving messages by Carlo to their old friends to say so, and to beg them not to be sorry for *them,* for, excepting that they would like some day to see those old friends again, they had nothing left to wish for in their new home:-

"And here the Tod story ends!" remarked Aunt Judy, in conclusion, "and I beg you to observe, No. 6, that, like all my stories, it ends happily. The children had now got hold of an amusement which was safe from interference, and which lasted - I am really afraid to say how long; for even after the fervour of their Tod love had abated, they found an endless source of invention and enjoyment in the cellar-home romance, and told each other anecdotes about it, from time to time, for more, I believe, than a year."

When Aunt Judy paused here, as if expecting some remark, all that No. 6 could say, was:-

"Poor little things!"

"Ay, they were still that," exclaimed Aunt Judy, "even in the midst of their new-found comfort. Oh, No. 6, when one thinks of the strange way in which they first of all created a sorrow for themselves, and then devised for themselves its consolation, what a pity it seems that no good was got out of it!"

It was not likely that No. 6 should guess what the good was which Aunt Judy thought might have been got out of it; and so she said; whereupon Aunt Judy explained:-

"Did it not offer a quite natural opportunity, - if any kind friend had but known of it, - of speaking to those children of some of the sacred hopes of our Christian faith? - of leading them, through kind talk about their own pretty fancies, to the subject of *what really becomes* of the dear friends who are taken away from us by death?

"Had I been *their* Aunt Judy," she continued, "I should have thought it no cruelty, but kindness then, to have spoken to them about their lost mother, and told them that she was living now in a place where she was much, much happier, than she had ever been before, and where one of the very few things she had left to

Mrs Alfred Gatty

wish for, was, that one day she might see them again: not in this world, where people are so often uncomfortable and sad, but in that happy one where there is no more sorrow, or crying, for God Himself wipes away the tears from all eyes.

"I should have told them besides," pursued Aunt Judy, "that it would not please their dear mother at all for them to fret for her, and *fancy they couldn't do without her,* and be discontented because God had taken her away, and think it would have been much better for them if He had not done so - (as if He did not know a thousand times better than they could do:) - but that it would please her very much for them to pray to God to make them good, so that they might all meet together at last in that very happy place.

"In short, No. 6, I would have led them, if possible, to make a comforting reality to themselves of the next world, as they had already got a comforting fancy out of the cellar-dream of the Tods. And that is the good, dear child, which I meant might have been got out of the Tod adventure."

Aunt Judy ceased, but there was no chance of seeing the effect of what she had said on No. 6's face, for it was laid on her sister's lap; probably to hide the tears which would come into her eyes at Aunt Judy's allusion to what she had said about *her.*

At last a rather husky voice spoke:-

"You can't expect people to like what is so very sad, even if it is - what you call - right - and all that." "No! neither does God expect it!" was Aunt Judy's earnest reply. "We are allowed to be sorry when trials come, for we feel the suffering, and cannot at present understand the blessing or necessity of it. But we are not allowed to 'sorrow without hope;' and we are not allowed, even when we are most sorry, to be rebellious, and fancy we could choose better for ourselves than God chooses for us."

Aunt Judy's lesson, as well as story, was ended now, and she began talking over the entertaining part of the Tod history, and then went on to other things, till No. 6 was quite herself again, and wanted to know how much was true about the motherless little girls; and when she found from Aunt Judy's answer that the account was by no means altogether an invention, she went into a fever-fidget to know who the children were, and what had become of them; and finally settled that the one thing in the world she most wished for, was to see them.

Nor would she be persuaded that this was a foolish idea, until Aunt Judy asked her how she would like to be introduced to a couple of *very* old women, with huge hooked noses, and beardy, nut-cracker chins, and be told that *those* were the motherless little girls who had broken their hearts over rabbits' tails! - an inquiry which tickled No. 6's fancy immensely, so that she began to laugh, and suggest a few additions of her own to the comical picture, in the course of doing which, she fortunately quite lost sight of the "one thing" which a few minutes before she had "most wished for in the world!"

"OUT OF THE WAY"

"Oh wonderful Son that can so astonish a Mother!"
HAMLET.

"What a horrid nuisance you are, No. 8, brushing everything down as you go by! Why can't you keep out of the way?"

"Oh, you mustn't come here, No. 8. Aunt Judy, look! he's sitting on my doll's best cloak. Do tell him to go away."

"I can't have you bothering me, No. 8; don't you see how busy I am, packing? Get away somewhere else."

"You should squeeze yourself into less than nothing, and be nowhere, No. 8."

The suggestion, (uttered with a jocose grin,) came from a small boy who had ensconced himself in the corner of a window, where he was sitting on his heels, painting the Union Jack of a ship in the *Illustrated London News*. He had certainly acted on the advice he gave, as nearly as was possible. Surely no little boy of his age ever got into so small a compass before, or in a position more effectually out of everybody's possible way. The window corner led nowhere, and there was nothing in it for anybody to want.

"No. 8, I never saw anything so tiresome as you are. Why will you poke your nose in where you're not wanted? You're always in the way."

"'He poked his flat nose into every place;'"

sung, *sotto voce,* by the small boy in the window corner.

No. 8 did not stop to dispute about it, though, in point of fact, his nose was not flat, so at least in that respect he did not resemble the duck in the song.

He had not, however, been successful in gaining the attention of his friends down-stairs, so he dawdled off to make an experiment in another quarter.

"Why, you're not coming into the nursery now, Master No. 8, surely! I can't do with you fidgetting about among all the clothes and packing. There isn't a minute to spare. You might keep out of the way till I've finished."

"Now, Master No. 8, you must be off. There's no time or room for you in the kitchen this morning. There's ever so many things to get ready yet. Run away as fast as you can."

"What *are* you doing in the passages, No. 8? Don't you see that you are in everybody's way? You had really better go to bed again."

But the speaker hurried forward, and No. 8 betook himself to the staircase, and sat down exactly in the middle of the middle flight. And there be amused himself by peeping through the banisters into the hall, where people were passing backwards and forwards in a great fuss; or listening to the talking and noise that were going on in the rooms above.

But be was not "out of the way" there, as he soon learnt. Heavy steps were presently heard along the landing, and heavy steps began to descend the stairs. Two men were carrying down a heavy trunk.

"You'll have to move, young gentleman, if you please," observed one; "you're right in the way just there!"

No. 8 descended with all possible speed, and arrived on the mat at the bottom.

"There now, I told you, you were always in the way," was the greeting he received. "How stupid it is! Try under the table, for pity's sake."

Under the table! it was not a bad idea; moreover, it was a new one - quite a fresh plan. No. 8 grinned and obeyed. The hall table was no bad asylum, after all, for a little boy who was always in the way everywhere else; besides, he could see everything that was going on. No. 8 crept under, and squatted himself on the cocoa-nut matting. He looked up, and looked round, and felt rather as if he was in a tent, only with a very substantial covering over his head.

Presently the dog passed by, and was soon coaxed to lie down in the table retreat by the little boy's side, and the two amused themselves very nicely together. The fact was, the family were going from home, and the least the little ones could do during the troublesome preparation, was not to be troublesome themselves; but this is sometimes rather a difficult thing for little ones to accomplish. Nevertheless, No. 8 had accomplished it at last.

"Capital, No. 8! you and the dog are quite a picture. If I had time, I would make a sketch of you."

That was the remark of the first person who went by afterwards, and No. 8 grinned as he heard it.

"Well done, No. 8! that's the best contrivance I ever saw!"

Remark the second, followed by a second grin.

"Why, you don't mean to say that you're under the table, Master No. 8? Well you *are* a good boy! I'm sure I'll tell your mamma."

Another grin.

"You dear old fellow, to put yourself so nicely out of the way! You're worth I don't know what."

Grin again.

"Master No. 8 under the table, to be sure! Well, and a very nice place it is, and quite suitable. Ever so much better than the hot kitchen, when there's baking and all sorts of things going on. Here, lovey! here's a little cake that was spared, that I was taking to the parlour; but, as you're there, you shall have it."

No. 8 grinned with all his heart this time.

"I wish I'd thought of that! Why, I could have painted my ship there without being squeezed!"

It needs scarcely to be told that this was the observation of the small boy who had watched an opportunity for emerging from the window corner without fuss, and was now carrying his little paint-box up-stairs to be packed away in the children's bag. As he spoke, he stooped down to look at No. 8 and the dog, and smiled his approbation, and No. 8 smiled in return.

"No. 8, how snug you do look!"

Once more an answering grin.

"No. 8, you're the best boy in the world; and if you stay there till Nurse is ready for you, you shall have a penny all to yourself."

No. 8's grin was accompanied by a significant nod this time, to show that he accepted the bargain.

"My darling No. 8, you may come out now. There! give me a kiss, and get dressed as fast as you can. The fly will be here directly. You're a very good boy indeed."

"No. 8, you're the pattern boy of the family, and I shall come with you in the fly, and tell you a story as we go along for a reward."

No. 8 liked both the praise, and the cake, and the penny, and the kiss, and the promise of the rewarding story for going under the table; but the why and wherefore of all these charming facts, was a complete mystery to him. What did that matter, however? He ran up-stairs, and got dressed, and was ready before anyone else; and, by a miracle of good fortune, was on the steps, and not in the middle of the carriage-drive, when the fly arrived, which was to take one batch of the large family party to the railway station.

No one was as fond of the fly conveyance as of the open carriage; for, in the first place, it was usually very full and stuffy; and, in the second, very little of the country could be seen from the windows.

But, on the present occasion, Aunt Judy having offered her services to accompany the fly detachment, there was a wonderful alteration of sentiment, as to who should be included. Aunt Judy, however, had her own ideas. The three little ones belonged to the fly, as it were by ancient usage and custom, and more than five it would not hold.

Five it would hold, however, and five accordingly got in, No. 4 having pleaded her own cause to be "thrown in:" and at last, with nurses and luggage and No. 5 outside, away they drove, leaving the open carriage and the rest to follow.

Nothing is perfect in this world. Those who had the airy drive missed the story, and regretted it; but it was fair that the pleasure should be divided.

And, after all, although the fly might be a little stuffy and closely packed, and although it cost some trouble to settle down without getting crushed, and make footstools of carpet bags, and let down all the windows, - the commotion was soon over; and it was a wonderful lull of peace and quietness, after the

Mrs Alfred Gatty

confusion and worry of packing and running about, to sit even in a rattling fly. And so for five minutes and more, all the travellers felt it to be, and a soothing silence ensued; some leaning back, others looking silently out at the retreating landscape, or studying with earnestness the wonderful red plush lining of the vehicle itself.

But presently, after the rest had lasted sufficiently long to recruit all the spirits, No. 7 remarked, not speaking to anybody in particular, "I thought Aunt Judy was going to tell us a story."

No. 7 was a great smiler in a quiet way, and he smiled now, as he addressed his remark to the general contents of the fly.

Aunt Judy laughed, and inquired for whom the observation was meant, adding her readiness to begin, if they would agree to sit quiet and comfortable, without shuffling up and down, or disputing about space and heat; and, these points being agreed to, she began her story as follows:-

"There were once upon a time a man and his wife who had an only son. They were Germans, I believe, for all the funny things that happen, happen in Germany, as you know by Grimm's fairy tales.

"Well! this man, Franz, had been a watchmaker and mender in an old-fashioned country town, and he had made such a comfortable fortune by the business, that he was able to retire before he grew very old; and so he bought a very pretty little villa in the outskirts of the town, had a garden full of flowers with a fountain in the middle, and enjoyed himself very much.

"His wife enjoyed herself too, but never so much as when the neighbours, as they passed by, peeped over the palings, and said, 'What a pretty place! What lucky people the watchmaker and his wife are! How they must enjoy themselves!'

"On such occasions, Madame Franz would run to her husband, crying out, 'Come here, my dear, as fast as you can! Come, and listen to the neighbours, saying, how we must enjoy ourselves!'

"Franz was very apt to grunt when his wife summoned him in this manner, and, at any rate, never would go as she requested; but little Franz, the son, who was very like his mother, and had got exactly her turn-up nose and sharp eyes, would scamper forward in a moment to hear what the neighbours had to say, and at the end would exclaim:-

"'Isn't it grand, mother, that everybody should think that?'

"To which his mother would reply:-

"'It is, Franz, dear! I'm so glad you feel for your mother!' and then the two would embrace each other very affectionately several times, and Madame Franz would go to her household business, rejoicing to think that, if her husband did not quite sympathize with her, her son did.

"Young Franz had been somewhat spoilt in his childhood, as only children generally are. As to his mother, from there being no brothers and sisters to compare him with, she thought such a boy had never been seen before; and she told old Franz so, so often, that at last he began to believe it too. And then they got all sorts of masters for him, to teach him everything they could think of, and qualify him, as his mother said, for some rich young lady to fall in love with. That was her idea of the way in which he was one day to make his fortune.

"At last, a time came when his mother thought the young gentleman quite finished and complete; fit for anything and anybody, and likely to create a sensation in the world. So she begged old Franz to dismiss all his masters, and give him a handsome allowance, that he might go off on his travels and make his fortune, in the manner before mentioned.

"Old Mr. Franz shook his head at first, and called it all a parcel of nonsense. Moreover, he declared that Master Franz was a mere child yet, and would get into a hundred foolish scrapes in less than a week; but mamma expressed her opinion so positively, and repeated it so often, that at last papa began to entertain it too, and gave his consent to the plan.

"The fact was, though I am sorry to say it, Mr. Franz was henpecked. That is, his wife was always trying to make him obey her, instead of obeying him, as she ought to have done; and she had managed him so long, that she knew she could persuade him, or talk him (which is much the same thing) into anything, provided she went on long enough.

"So she went on about Franz going off on his travels with a handsome allowance, till Papa Franz consented, and settled an income upon him, which, if they had been selfish parents, they would have said they could not afford; but, as it was, they talked the matter over together, and told each other that it was very little two old souls like themselves would want when their gay son was away; and so they would draw in, and live quite quietly, as they used to do in their early days before they grew rich, and would let the lad have the money to spend upon his amusements.

"Young Franz either didn't know, or didn't choose to think about this. Clever as he was about many things, he was not clever enough to take in the full value of the sacrifices his parents were making for him; so he thanked them lightly for the promised allowance, rattled the first payment cheerfully into his purse, and smiled on papa and mamma with almost condescending complacency. When he was equipped in his best suit, and just ready for starting, his mother took him aside.

"'Franz, my dear,' she said, 'you know how much money and pains have been spent on your education. You can play, and dance, and sing, and talk, and make yourself heard wherever you go. Now mind you do make yourself heard, or who is to find out your merits? Don't be shy and downcast when you come among strangers. All you have to think about, with your advantages, is to make yourself agreeable. That's the rule for you! Make yourself agreeable wherever you go, and the wife and the fortune will soon be at your feet. And, Franz,' continued she, laying hold of the button of his coat, 'there is something else. You know, I have often said that the one only thing I could wish different about you is, that your nose should not turn up quite so much. But you see, my darling boy, we can't alter our noses. Nevertheless, look here! you can incline your head in such a manner as almost to hide the little defect. See - this way - there - let me put

Mrs Alfred Gatty

it as I mean - a little down and on one side. It was the way I used to carry my head before I married, or I doubt very much whether your father would have looked my way. Think of this when you're in company. It's a graceful attitude too, and you will find it much admired.'

"Franz embraced his mother, and promised obedience to all her commands; but he was glad when her lecture ended, for he was not very fond of her remarks upon his nose. Just then the door of his father's room opened, and he called out:-

"'Franz, my dear, I want to speak to you.'

"Franz entered the room, and 'Now, my dear boy,' said papa, 'before you go, let me give you one word of parting advice; but stop, we will shut the door first, if you please. That's right. Well, now, look here. I know that no pains or expense have been spared over your education. You can play, and dance, and sing, and talk, and make yourself heard wherever you go.'

"'My dear sir,' interrupted Franz, 'I don't think you need trouble yourself to go on. My mother has just been giving me the advice beforehand.'

"'No, has she though?' cried old Franz, looking up in his son's face; but then he shook his head, and said:-

"'No, she hasn't, Franz; no, she hasn't; so listen to me. We've all made a fuss about you, and praised whatever you've done, and you've been a sort of idol and wonder among us. But, now you're going among strangers, you will find yourself Mr. Nobody, and the great thing is, you must be contented to be Mr. Nobody at first. Keep yourself in the background, till people have found out your merits for themselves; and never get into anybody's way. Keep *out* of the way, in fact, that's the safest rule. It's the secret of life for a young man - How impatient you look! but mark my words:- all you have to attend to, with your advantages, is, to keep out of the way.'

"After this bit of advice, the father bestowed his blessing on his dear Franz, and unlocked the door, close to which they found Mrs. Franz, waiting rather impatiently till the conference was over.

"'What a time you have been, Franz!' she began; but there was no time to talk about it, for they all knew that the coach, or post-wagon, as they call it in Germany, was waiting.

"Mrs. Franz wrung her son's hand.

"'Remember what I've said, my dearest Franz!' she cried.

"'Trust me!' was Mr. Franz's significant reply.

"'You'll not forget my rule?' whispered papa.

"'Forget, sir? no, that's not possible,' answered

Mr. Franz in a great hurry, as he ran off to catch the post-wagon; for they could see it in the distance beginning to move, though part of the young gentleman's luggage was on board.

"Well! he was just in time; but what do you think was the next thing he did, after keeping the people waiting? A sudden thought struck him, that it would be as well for the driver and passengers to know how well educated he had been, so he began to give the driver a few words of geographical information about the roads they were going.

"'Jump in directly, sir, if you please,' was the driver's gruff reply.

"'Certainly not, till I've made you understand what I mean,' says Master Franz, quite facetiously. But, then, smack went the whip, and the horses gave a jolt forwards, and over the tip of the learned young gentleman's foot went the front wheel.

"It was a nasty squeeze, though it might have been worse, but Franz called out very angrily, something or other about 'disgraceful carelessness,' on which the driver smacked his whip again, and shouted:-

"'Gentlemen that won't keep out of the way, must expect to have their toes trodden on.' Everybody laughed at this, but Franz was obliged to spring inside, without taking any notice of the joke, as the coach was now really going on; and if he had began to talk, he would have been left behind.

"And now," continued Aunt Judy, stopping herself, "while Franz is jolting along to the capital town of the country, you shall tell me whose advice you think he followed when he got to the end of the journey, and began life for himself - his father's or his mother's?"

There was a universal cry, mixed with laughter, of "His mother's!"

"Quite right," responded Aunt Judy. "His mother's, of course. It was far the most agreeable, no doubt. Keeping out of the way is a rather difficult thing for young folks to manage."

A glance at No. 8 caused that young gentleman's face to grin all over, and Aunt Judy proceeded:-

"After his arrival at the great hotel of the town, he found there was to be a public dinner there that evening, which anybody might go to, who chose to pay for it; and this he thought would be a capital opportunity for him to begin life: so, accordingly, he went up-stairs to dress himself out in his very best clothes for the occasion.

"And then it was that, as he sat in front of the glass, looking at his own face, while he was brushing his hair and whiskers, and brightening them up with bear's-grease, he began to think of his father and mother, and what they had said, and what he had best do.

"'An excellent, well-meaning couple, of course, but as old-fashioned as the clocks they used to mend,' was his first thought. 'As to papa, indeed, the poor old gentleman thinks the world has stood still since he was a young man, thirty years ago. His stiff notions were all very well then, perhaps, but in these advanced times they are perfectly quizzical. Keep out of the way, indeed! Why, any ignoramus can do that, I should think! Well, well, he means well, all the same, so one must not be severe. As to mamma now - poor thing - though she *is* behindhand herself in many ways, yet she *does* know a good thing when she sees it, and that's a great point. She can appreciate the probable results of my very superior education and appearance.

To be sure, she's a little silly over that nose affair; - but women will always be silly about something.'

"Nevertheless, at this point in his meditations, Master Franz might have been seen inclining his head down on one side, just as his mother had recommended, and then giving a look at the mirror, to see whether the vile turn-up did really disappear in that attitude. I suspect, however, that he did not feel quite satisfied about it, for he got rather cross, and finished his dressing in a great hurry, but not before he had settled that there could be only one opinion as to whose advice he should be guided by - dear mamma's.

"'Should it fail,' concluded he to himself, as he gave the last smile at the looking-glass, 'there will be poor papa's old-world notion to fall back upon, after all.'

"Now, you must know that Master Franz had never been at one of these public dinners before, so there is no denying that when he entered the large dining-hall, where there was a long table, set out with plates, and which was filling fast with people, not one of whom he knew, he felt a little confused. But he repeated his mother's words softly to himself, and took courage: *'Don't be shy and downcast when you come among strangers. All you have to think about, with your advantages, is to make yourself agreeable;'* and, on the strength of this, he passed by the lower end of the table, where there were several unoccupied places, and walked boldly forward to the upper end, where groups of people were already seated, and were talking and laughing together.

"In the midst of one of these groups, there was one unoccupied seat, and in the one next to it sat a beautiful, well-dressed young lady. 'Why, this is the very thing,' thought Mr. Franz to himself. 'Who knows but what this is the young lady who is to make my fortune?'

"There was a card, it is true, in the plate in front of the vacant seat, but 'as to that,' thought Franz, 'first come, first served, I suppose; I shall sit down!'

"And sit down the young gentleman accordingly did in the chair by the beautiful young lady, and even bowed and smiled to her as he did so.

"But the next instant he was tapped on the shoulder by a waiter.

"'The place is engaged, sir!' and the man pointed to the card in the plate.

"'Oh, if that's all,' was Mr. Franz's witty rejoinder, 'here's another to match!' and thereupon he drew one of his own cards from his pocket, threw it into the plate, and handed the first one to the astonished waiter, with the remark:-

"'The place is engaged, my good friend, you see!'

"The young goose actually thought this impudence clever, and glanced across the table for applause as he spoke. But although Mamma Watchmaker, if she had heard it, might have thought it a piece of astonishing wit, the strangers at the public table were quite of a different opinion, and there was a general cry of 'Turn him out!'

"'Turn me out!' shouted Mr. Franz, jumping up from

his chair, as if he intended to fight them all round; and there is no knowing what more nonsense he might not have talked, but that a very sonorous voice behind him called out, - a hand laying hold of him by the shoulders at the same time -

"'Young man, I'll trouble you to get out of my chair, and' (a little louder) 'out of my way, and' (a little louder still) 'to *keep* out of my way!'

"Franz felt himself like a child in the grasp of the man who spoke; and one glimpse he caught of a pair of coal-black eyes, two frowning eye-brows, and a moustachioed mouth, nearly frightened him out of his wits, and he was half way down the room before he knew what was happening; for, after the baron let him go, the waiter seized him and hustled him along, till he came to the bottom of the table; where, however, there was now no room for him, as all the vacant places had been filled up; so he was pushed finally to a side-table in a corner, at which sat two men in foreign dresses, not one word of whose language he could understand.

"These two fellows talked incessantly together too, which was all the more mortifying, because they gesticulated and laughed as if at some capital joke. Franz was very quiet at first, for the other adventure had sobered him, but presently, with his mother's advice running in his head, he resolved to make himself agreeable, if possible.

"So, at the next burst of merriment, he affected to have entered into the joke, threw himself back in his chair and laughed as loudly as they did. The men stared for a second, then frowned, and then one of them shouted something to him very loudly, which he did not understand; so he placed his hand on his heart, put on an expressive smile, and offered to shake hands. Thought he, that will be irresistible! But he was mistaken. The other man now called loudly to the waiter, and a moment after, Franz found himself being conveyed by the said waiter through the doorway into the hall, with the remark resounding in his ears:-

"'What a foolish young gentleman you must be! Why can't you keep out of people's way?'

"'My good friend,' cried Mr. Franz, 'that's not my plan at present. I'm trying to make myself agreeable.'

"'Oh - pooh! - bother agreeable,' cried the waiter. 'What's the use of making yourself agreeable, if you're always in the way? Here! - step back, sir! don't you see the tray coming?'

"Franz had not noticed it, and would probably have got a thump on the head from it, if his friend the waiter had not pulled him back. The man was a real good-natured, smiling German, and said:-

"'Come, young gentleman, here's a candle; - you've a bed-room here, of course. Now, you take my advice, and go to bed. You *will* be out of the way there, and perhaps you'll get up wiser to-morrow.'

"Franz took the candlestick mechanically, but, said he:-

"'I understood there was to be dancing here tonight, and I can dance, and - '

"'Oh, pooh! bother dancing,' interrupted the waiter.

'What's the use of dancing, if you're to be in everybody's way, and I know you will; you can't help it. Here, be advised for once, and go to bed. I'll bring you up some coffee before long. Go quietly up now - mind. Good night.'

"Two minutes afterwards, Mr. Franz found himself walking up-stairs, as the waiter had ordered him to do, though he muttered something about 'officious fellow' as he went along.

"And positively he went to bed, as the officious fellow recommended; and while he lay there waiting for the coffee, he began wondering what *could* be the cause of the failure of his attempts to make himself agreeable. Surely his mother was right - surely there could be no doubt that, with his advantages - but he did not go on with the sentence.

"Well, after puzzling for some time, a bright thought struck him. It was entirely owing to that stupid nose affair, which his mother was so silly about. Of course that was it! He had done everything else she recommended, but he could not keep his head down at the same time, so people saw the snub! Well, he would practise the attitude now, at any rate, till the coffee came!

"No sooner said than done. Out of bed jumped Mr. Franz, and went groping about for the table to find matches to light the candle. But, unluckily, he had forgotten how the furniture stood, so he got to the door by a mistake, and went stumbling up against it, just as the waiter with the coffee opened it on the other side.

"There was a plunge, a shout, a shuffling of feet, and

then both were on the floor, as was also the hot coffee, which scalded Franz's bare legs terribly.

"The waiter got up first, and luckily it was the 'officious fellow' with the smiling face. And said he:-

"'What a miserable young man you must be, to be sure! Why, you're *never* out of the way, not even when you're gone to bed!'

This last anecdote caused an uproar of delight in the fly, and so much noise, that Aunt Judy had to call the party to order, and talk about the horses being frightened, after which she proceeded:-

"I am sorry to say Mr. Franz did not get up next morning as much wiser as the waiter had expected, for he laid all the blame of his misfortunes on his nose instead of his impertinence, and never thought of correcting himself, and being less intrusive.

"On the contrary, after practising holding his head down for ten minutes before the glass, he went out to the day's amusements, as saucy and confident as ever.

"Now there is no time," continued Aunt Judy, "for my telling you all Mr. Franz's funny scrapes and adventures. When we get to the end of the journey, you must invent some for yourselves, and sit together, and tell them in turns, while we are busy unpacking. I will only just say, that wherever he went, the same sort of things happened to him, because he was always thrusting himself forward, and always getting pushed back in consequence.

"Out of the public gardens he got fairly turned at last,

Mrs Alfred Gatty

because he would talk politics to some strange gentlemen on a bench. They got up and walked away, but, five minutes afterwards, a very odd-looking man looked over Franz's shoulder, and said significantly, 'I recommend you to leave these gardens, sir, and walk elsewhere.' And poor Franz, who had heard of such things as prisons and dungeons for political offenders, felt a cold shudder run through him, and took himself off with all possible speed, not daring to look behind him, for fear he should see that dreadful man at his heels. Indeed, he never felt safe till he was in his bed-room again, and had got the waiter to come and talk to him.

"'Dear me,' said the waiter, 'what a very silly young gentleman you must be, to go talking away without being asked!'

"'But,' said Franz, 'you don't consider what a superior education I have had. I can talk and make myself heard - '

"'Oh, pooh! bother talking,' interrupted the waiter; 'what's the use of talking when nobody wants to listen? Much better go to bed.'

"Franz would not give in yet, but was comforted to find the waiter did not think he would be thrown into prisons and dungeons; so he dined, and dressed, and went to the theatre to console himself, where however he *made himself heard* so effectually - first applauding, then hissing, and even speaking his opinions to the people round him - that a set of young college students combined together to get rid of him, and, I am sorry to add, they made use of a little kicking as the surest plan; and so, before half the play was over, Mr. Franz found himself in the street!

"Now, then, I have told you enough of Mr. Franz's follies, except the one last adventure, which made him alter his whole plan of proceeding.

"He had had two letters of introduction to take with him: one to an old partner of his father's, who had settled in the capital some years before; another to some people of more consequence, very distant family connections. And, of course, Mr. Franz went there first, as there seemed a nice chance of making his fortune among such great folks.

"And really the great folks would have been civil enough, but that he soon spoilt everything by what *he* called 'making himself agreeable.' He was too polite, too affectionate, too talkative, too instructive, by half! He assured the young ladies that he approved very highly of their singing; trilled out a little song of his own, unasked, at his first visit; fondled the pet lap-dog on his knee; congratulated papa on looking wonderfully well for his age; asked mamma if she had tried the last new spectacles; and, in short, gave his opinions, and advice, and information, so freely, that as soon as he was gone the whole party exclaimed:-

"'What an impertinent jackanapes!' a jackanapes being nothing more nor less than a human monkey.

"This went on for some time, for he called very often, being too stupid, in spite of his supposed cleverness, to take the hints that were thrown out, that such repeated visits were not wanted.

"At last, however, the family got desperate and one

morning when he arrived, (having teazed them the day before for a couple of hours,) he saw nobody in the drawing-room when he was ushered in.

"Never mind, thought he, they'll be here directly when they know *I'm* come! And having brought a new song in his pocket, which he had been practising to sing to them, he sat down to the piano, and began performing alone, thinking how charmed they would be to hear such beautiful sounds in the distance!

"But, in the middle of his song, he heard a discordant shout, and jumping up, discovered the youngest little Missy hid behind the curtain, and crying tremendously.

"Mr. Franz became quite theatrical. 'Lovely little pet, where are your sisters? Have they left my darling to weep alone?'

"'They shut the door before I could get through,' sobbed the lovely little pet; 'and I won't be your darling a bit!'

"Mr. Franz laughed heartily, and said how clever she was, took her on his knee, told her her sisters would be back again directly, and finished his remark by a kiss.

"Unfortunate Mr. Franz! The young lady immediately gave him an unmistakable box on the ear with her small fist, and vociferated

"No, they won't, they won't, they won't! They'll never come back till you're gone! They've gone away to get out of *your* way, because you won't keep out of *theirs*. And you're a forward puppy, papa says, and can't take a hint; and you're always in everybody's way, and *I'll* get out of your way, too!'

"Here the little girl began to kick violently; but there was no occasion. Mr. Franz set her down, and while she ran off to her sisters, he rushed back to the hotel, and double-locked himself into his room.

"After a time, however, he sent for his friend the waiter, for he felt that a talk would do him good.

"But the 'officious fellow' shook his head terribly.

"'How many more times am I to tell you what a foolish young gentleman you are?' cried he. 'Will you never get up wiser any morning of the year?'

"'I thought,' murmured Franz, in broken, almost sobbing accents - 'I thought - the young ladies - would have been delighted - with - my song; - you see - I've been - so well taught - and I can sing - '

"'Oh! pooh, pooh, pooh!' interrupted the waiter once more. 'Bother singing and everything else, if you've not been asked! Much better go to bed!'

"Poor Franz! It was hard work to give in, and he made a last effort.

"'Don't you think - after all - that the prejudice - is owing to - what I told you about:- people do so dislike a snub-nose?'

"'Oh, pooh! bother a snub-nose,' exclaimed the waiter; 'what will your nose signify, if you don't poke it in everybody's way?'

Mrs Alfred Gatty

"And with this conclusion Mr. Franz was obliged to be content; and he ordered his dinner up-stairs, and prepared himself for an evening of tears and repentance.

"But, before the waiter had been gone five minutes, he returned with a letter in his hand.

"'Now, here's somebody asking something at last,' said he, for a servant had brought it.

"Franz trembled as he took it. It was sure to be either a scolding or a summons to prison, he thought. But no such thing: it was an invitation to dinner. Franz threw it on the floor, and kicked it from him - he would go nowhere - see nobody any more!

"The 'officious fellow' picked it up, and read it. 'Mr. Franz,' said he, 'you mustn't go to bed this time: you must go to this dinner instead. It's from your father's old partner - he wishes you had called, but as you haven't called, he asks you to dine. Now you're wanted, Mr. Franz, and must go.'

"'I shall get into another mess,' cried Franz, despondingly.

"'Oh, pooh! you've only to keep out of everybody's way, and all will be right,' insisted the waiter, as he left the room.

"'Only to keep out of everybody's way, and all will be right,' ejaculated Mr. Franz, as he looked at his crest-fallen face in the glass. 'It's a strange rule for getting on in life! However,' continued he, cheering up, 'one plan has failed, and it's only fair to give the other a chance!'

"And all the rest of dressing-time, and afterwards as he walked along the streets, he kept repeating his father's words softly to himself, which was at first a very difficult thing to do, because he could not help mixing them up with his mother's. It was the funniest thing in the world to hear him: '*All you have to attend to, with your advantages is to - make yourself* - no, no! not to make myself agreeable - *is to - keep out of the way!* - that's it!' (with a sigh.)

"When Franz arrived at the house, he rang the bell so gently, that he had to ring twice before he was heard; and then they concluded it was some beggar, who was afraid of giving a good pull.

"So, when he was ushered into the drawing-room, the old partner came forward to meet him, took him by both hands, and, after one look into his downcast face, said:-

"'My dear Mr. Franz, you must put on a bolder face, and ring a louder peal, next time you come to the house of your father's old friend!'

"Mr. Franz answered this warm greeting by a sickly smile, and while he was being introduced to the family, kept bowing on, thinking of nothing but how he was to keep out of everybody's way!'

"He was tempted every five minutes, of course, to break out in his usual style, and could have found it in his heart to chuck the whole party under the chin, and take all the talk to himself. But he could be determined enough when he chose; and having determined to give his father's rule a fair chance, he restrained himself to the utmost.

"So, not even the hearty reception of the old partner and his wife, nor the smiling faces of either daughters or sons, could lure him into opening out. 'Yes' and 'No;' 'Do you think so?' 'I dare say;' 'Perhaps;' 'No doubt you're right;' and other such unmeaning little phrases were all he would utter when they talked to him.

"'How shy he is, poor fellow!' thought the ladies, and then they talked to him all the more. One tried to amuse him with one subject, another with another. How did he like the public gardens? Were they not very pretty? - He scarcely knew. No doubt they were, if *they* thought so. What did he think of the theatre? - It was very hot when he was there. Had he any friends in the town? - He couldn't say friends - he knew one or two people a little. And the poor youth could hardly restrain a groan, as he answered each of the questions.

"Then they chatted of books, and music, and dancing, and pressed him hard to discover what he knew, and could do, and liked best; and when it oozed out even from his short answers, that he had read certain books in more than one language, and could sing - just a little; and dance - just a little; and do several other things - just a little, too, all sorts of nods and winks passed through the family, and they said:-

"'Ah, when you know us better, and are not so shy of us as strangers, we shall find out you are as clever again as you pretend to be, dear Mr. Franz!'

"'I'll tell you what,' added the old partner, coming up

at this moment, 'it's a perfect treat to me, Mr. Franz, to have a young man like you in my house! You're your father over again, and I can't praise you more. He was the most modest, unobtrusive man in all our town, and yet knew more of his business than all of us put together.'

"'No, no, I can't allow that,' cried the motherly wife.

"'Nonsense!' replied the old partner. 'However, my dear boy - for I really must call you so - it was that very thing that made your father's fortune; I mean that he was just as unpretending as he was clever. Everybody trusts an unpretending man. And *you'll* make your fortune too in the same manner, trust me, before long. Now, boys!' added he, turning to his sons, 'you hear what I say, and mind you take the hint! As for the young puppies of the present day, who fancy themselves fit to sit in the chair of their elders as soon as ever they have learnt their alphabet, and are for thrusting themselves forward in every company - Mr. Franz, I'll own it to you, because you will understand me - I have no patience with such rude, impertinent Jackanapeses, and always long to kick them down-stairs.'

"The old partner stood in front of Mr. Franz as he spoke, and clenched his fist in animation. Mr. Franz sat on thorns. He first went hot, and then he went cold - he felt himself kicked down-stairs as he listened - he was ready to cry - he was ready to fight - he was ready to run away - he was ready to drop on his knees, and confess himself the very most impertinent of all the impertinent Jackanapes' race.

But he gulped, and swallowed, and shut his teeth close,

and nobody found him out; only he looked very pale, which the good mother soon noticed, and said she to her husband:-

"'My dear love, don't you see how fagged and weary it makes Mr. Franz look, to hear you raving on about a parcel of silly lads with whom *he* has nothing in common? You will frighten him out of his wits.'

"'Mr. Franz will forgive me, I know,' cried the old partner, gently. 'Jacintha, my dear, fetch the wine and cake!'

"The kind, careful souls feared he was delicate, and insisted on his having some refreshment; and then papa ordered the young people to give their guest some music; and Franz sat by while the sons and daughters went through a beautiful opera chorus, which was so really charming, that Mr. Franz did forget himself for a minute, clapped violently, and got half-way through the word 'encore' in a very loud tone. But he checked himself instantly, coloured, apologized for his rudeness, and retreated further back from the piano.

"Of course, this new symptom of modesty was met by more kindness, and followed by a sly hint from the merry Jacintha, that Mr. Franz's turn for singing had come now!

"Poor Mr. Franz! with the recollection of the morning's adventure on his mind, and his father's rule ringing in his ears, he felt singing to be out of the question, so he declined. On which they entreated, insisted, and would listen to no refusal. And Jacintha went to him, and looked at him with her sweetest smile, and said, 'But you know, Mr. Franz, you said you could sing a little; and if it's ever so little, you should sing *when you're asked*!' and with that Miss Jacintha offered him her hand, and led him to the piano.

"Franz was annoyed, though he ought to been pleased.

"'But how *am* I to keep out of people's way,' thought he to himself, 'if they will pull me forward? It's the oddest thing I ever knew. I can't do right either way.'

"Then a thought struck him:-

"'I have no music, Miss Jacintha,' said he, 'and I can't sing without music;' and he was going back again to his chair in the corner.

"'But we have all the new music,' was her answer, and she opened a portfolio at once. 'See, here's the last new song!' and she held one up before the unfortunate youth, who at the sight of it coloured all over, even to the tips of his ears. Whereupon Miss Jacintha, who was watching him, laughed, and said she had felt sure he knew it; and down she sat, and began to play the accompaniment, and in two minutes afterwards Mr. Franz found himself - in spite of himself, as it were - exhibiting in *the* song, the fatal song of the morning's adventure.

"It was a song of tender sentiment, and the singer's almost tremulous voice added to the effect, and a warm clapping of hands greeted its conclusion.

"But by that time Mr. Franz was so completely exhausted with the struggles of this first effort on the new plan, that he began to wish them good-night, saying he would not intrude upon them any longer.

"They would shake hands with him, though he tried to bow himself off without; and the old partner followed him down-stairs into the hall.

"'Mr. Franz,' said he, 'we have been delighted to make your acquaintance, but this has been only a quiet family party. Now we know your *sort,* you must come again, and meet our friends. Wife will fix the day, and send you word; and don't you be afraid, young man! Mind you come, and put your best foot forward among us all!'

"Franz was almost desperate. His conscience began to reproach him. What! was he going to accept all this kindness, like a rogue receiving money under false pretences? He was shocked, and began to protest:-

"'I assure you, dear sir, I don't deserve - You are quite under a mistake - I really am not - the fact is, you think a great deal better of me than - "

"'Nonsense!' shouted the old partner, clapping him vigorously on the back. 'Why, you're not going to teach me at my time of life, surely? Not going to turn as conceited as that, after all, eh? Come, come, Mr. Franz, no nonsense! And to-morrow,' he added, 'I'll send you letters of introduction to some of my friends, who will show you the lions, and make much of you. You will be well received wherever you take them, first for my sake, and afterwards for your own. There, there! I won't hear a word! No thanks - I hate them! Good night.'

"And the old partner fairly pushed Mr. Franz through

the door.

"'Oh dear, oh dear!' was the waiter's exclamation when Franz reached the hotel, and the light of the lamp shone on his white, worn-out face. 'Oh dear, oh dear! I fear you've been a silly young gentleman over again! What *have* you been doing this time?'

"'I've been trying to keep out of everybody's way all the evening,' growled Mr. Franz, 'and they would pull me forward, in spite of myself.'

"'No - really though?' cried the waiter, as if it were scarcely possible.

"'Really,' sighed poor Mr. Franz.

"'Then do me the honour, sir,' exclaimed the waiter, with a sudden deference of manner; and taking the tips of Franz's fingers in his own, he bent over them with a salute. 'You're a wise young gentleman now, sir, and your fortune's made. I'm glad you've hit it at last!

"And Mr. Franz had hit it at last, indeed," continued Aunt Judy, "as appeared more plainly still by the letters of introduction which reached him next morning. They were left open, and were to this effect:-

"' . . . The bearer of this is the son of an old friend. One of the most agreeable young men I ever saw. As modest as he is well educated, and I can't say more. Procure him some amusement, that a little of his shyness may be rubbed off; and forward his fortunes, my dear friend, as far as you can . . . '

"Franz handed one of these letters to his friend the

waiter, and the 'officious fellow' grinned from ear to ear.

"'There is only one more thing to fear,' observed he.

"'And what?' asked Franz.

"'Why, that now you're comfortable, my dear young gentleman, your head should be turned, and you should begin to make yourself agreeable again, and spoil all.'

"'Oh, pooh! bother agreeable; *I* say now, as you did,' cried Franz, laughing. 'No, no, my good friend, I'm not going to make myself agreeable any more. I know better than that at last!'

"'Then your fortune's safe as well as made!' was the waiter's last remark, as he was about to withdraw: but Franz followed him to the door.

"'I found out a rather curious thing this evening, do you know!'

"'And that was? - ' inquired his humble friend.

"'Why, that I was sitting all the time in that very attitude my mother recommended - with my head a little down, you know - so that I really don't think they noticed my snub.'

"The waiter got as far as, 'Oh, pooh!' but Franz was nervous, and interrupted him.

"'Yes - yes! I don't believe there's anything in it myself; but it will be a comfort to my mother to think it was her advice that made my fortune, which she will do when I tell her that!'

"'Ah! - the ladies will be romantic now and then!' exclaimed the waiter, with a flourish of his hand, 'and you must trim the comfort to a person's taste.'

"And in due time," pursued Aunt Judy, "that was exactly what Mr. Franz did. Strictly adhering to his father's rule, and encouraged by its capital success that first night, he got so out of the habit of being pert, and foolish, and inconsiderate, that he ended by never having any wish to be so; so that he really became what the old partner had imagined him to be at first. It was a great restraint for some time, but his modest manners fitted him at last as easy as an old shoe, and he was welcome at every house, because he was *never in the way,* and always knew when to retire!

"It was a jovial day for Papa and Mamma's Watch-maker when, two years afterwards, Mr. Franz returned home, a partner in the old partner's prospe-rous business, and with the smiling Jacintha for his bride.

"And then, in telling his mother of that first evening of his good fortune, he did not forget to mention that he had hung down his head all the time, as she had advised; and, just as he expected, she jumped up in the most extravagant delight.

"'I knew how it would be all along!' cried she; 'I told you so! I knew if you could only hide that terrible snub all would be well; and I'm sure our pretty Jacintha wouldn't have looked your way if you hadn't! See, now! you have to thank your mother for it all!'

"Franz was quite happy himself, so he smiled, and let his mother be happy her way too; but he opened his heart of hearts to poor old-fashioned papa, and told him - well, in fact, all his follies and mistakes, and their cure. And if mamma was happy in her bit of comfort, papa was not less so in his, for there is not a more delightful thing in the world than for father and son to understand each other as friends; and old Franz would sometimes walk up and down in his room, listening to the cheerful young voices up-stairs, and say to himself, that if Mother Franz - good soul as she was - did not always quite enter into his feelings, it was his comfort to be blessed with a son who did!"

* * *

What a long story it had been! Aunt Judy was actually tired out when she got to the end, and could not talk about it, but the little ones did till they arrived at the station, and had to get out.

And in the evening, when they were all sitting together before they went to bed, there was no small discussion about the story of Mr. Franz, and how people were to know what was really good manners - when to come forward, and when to hold back - and the children were a little startled at first, when their mother told them that the best rules for good manners were to be found in the Bible.

But when she reminded them of that text, "When thou art bidden, go and sit down in the lowest room," &c. they saw in those words a very serious reason for not pushing forward into the best place in company. And when they recollected that every man was to do to others as he wished others to do to him, it became clear to them that it was the duty of all people to study their neighbours' comfort and pleasure as well as their own; and it was no hard matter to show how this rule applied to all the little ins and outs of every-day life, whether at home, or in society. And there were plenty of other texts, ordering deference to elders, and the modesty which arises out of that humility of spirit which "vaunteth not itself," and "is not puffed up." There was, moreover, the comfortable promise, that "the meek" should "inherit the earth."

Of course, it was difficult to the little ones, just at first, to see how such very serious words could apply to anybody's manners, and especially to their own.

But it was a difficulty which mamma, with a little explanation, got over very easily; and before the little ones went to bed, they quite understood that in restraining themselves from teazing and being troublesome, they were not only not being "tiresome," but were actually obeying several Gospel rules.

"NOTHING TO DO."

"Had I a little son, I would christen him NOTHING-TO-DO."
         CHARLES LAMB.

There is a complaint which is not to be found in the doctor's books, but which is, nevertheless, such a common and troublesome one, that one heartily wishes some physic could be discovered which would cure it.

It may be called the *nothing-to-do* complaint.

Even quite little children are subject to it, but they never have it badly. Parents and nurses have only to give them something to do, or tell them of something to do, and the thing is put right. A puzzle or a picture-book relieves the attack at once.

But after the children have out-grown puzzles, and picture-books, and nurses, and when even a parent's advice is received with a little impatience, then the *nothing-to-do* complaint, if it seizes them at all, is a serious disease, and often very difficult to cure; and, if not cured, alas! then follows the melancholy spectacle of grown-up men and women, who are a plague to their friends, and a weariness to themselves; because, living under the notion that there is *nothing* for them *to do,* they want everybody else to do something to amuse them.

Anyone can laugh at the old story of the gentleman who got into such a fanciful state of mind - hypo-chondriacal, it is called - that he thought he was his own umbrella; and so, on coming in from a walk, would go and lay *it* in the easy-chair by the fire, while he himself went and leant up against the wall in a corner of the hall.

But this gentleman was not a bit more fanciful and absurd than the people, whether young or old, who look out of windows on rainy days and groan because there is *nothing to do;* when, in reality, there is so much for everybody to do, that most people leave half their share undone.

The oddest part of the complaint is, that it generally comes on worst in those who from being comfortably off in the world, and from having had a great deal of education, have such a variety of things to do, that one would fancy they could never be at a loss for a choice.

But these are the very people who are most afflicted. It is always the young people who have books, and leisure, and music, and drawing, and gardens, and pleasure-grounds, and villagers to be kind to, who lounge to the rain-bespattered windows on a dull morning, and groan because there is *nothing to do.*

In justice to girls in general, it should be here mentioned, that they are on the whole less liable to the complaint than the young lords of the creation, who are supposed to be their superiors in sense. Philosophers may excuse this as they please, but the fact remains,

Mrs Alfred Gatty

that there are few large families in England, whose sisterhoods have not at times been teazed half out of their wits, by the growlings of its young gentlemen, during paroxysms of the *nothing-to-do* complaint; growling being one of its most characteristic symptoms.

Perhaps among all the suffering sisterhoods it would have been difficult to find a young lady less liable to catch such a disorder herself, than Aunt Judy; and perhaps that was the reason why she used to do such tremendous battle with No. 3, whenever, after his return from school for the holidays, he happened to have an attack.

"What are you groaning at through the window, No. 3?" she inquired on one such occasion; "is it raining?"

A very gruff-sounding "No," was the answer - No. 3 not condescending to turn round as he spoke. He proceeded, however, to state that it had rained when he got up, and he supposed it would rain again as a matter-of-course, (for his especial annoyance being implied,) and he concluded:-

"It's so horribly 'slow' here, with nothing to do."

No. 6, who was sitting opposite Aunt Judy, doing a French exercise, here looked up at her sister, and perceiving a smile steal over her face, took upon herself to think her brother's remark very ridiculous, so, said she, with a saucy giggle:-

"I can find you plenty to do, No. 3, in a minute. Come and write my French exercise for me.

No. 3 turned sharply round at this, with a frown on his face which by no means added to its beauty, and called out:-

"Now, Miss Pert, I recommend you to hold your tongue. I don't want any advice from a conceited little minx like you."

Miss Pert was extinguished at once, and set to work at the French exercise again most industriously, and a general silence ensued.

But people in the nothing-to-do complaint are never quiet for long. Teazing is quite as constant a symptom of it, as growling, so No. 3 soon came lounging from the window to the table, and began:-

"I say, Judy, I wish you would put those tiresome books, and drawings, and rubbish away, and I think of something to do."

"But it's the books, and the drawings, and the rubbish that give me something to do," cried Aunt Judy. "You surely don't expect me to give them up, and go arm and arm with you round the house, bemoaning the slowness of our fate which gives us nothing to do. Or shall we? Come, I don't care; I will if you like. But which shall we complain to first, mamma, or the maids?"

While she was saying this, Aunt Judy shut up her drawing book, jumped up from her chair, drew No. 3's arm under her own, and repeated:-

"Come! which? mamma, or the maids?" while Miss Pert opposite was labouring with all her might to smother the laugh she dared not indulge in.

But No. 3 pushed Aunt Judy testily away.

"'Nonsense, Judy! what has that to do with it? It's all very well for you girls - now, Miss Pert, mind your own affairs, and don't stare at me! - to amuse yourself with all manner of - "

"Follies, of course," cried Aunt Judy, laughing, "don't be afraid of speaking out, No. 3. It's all very well for us girls to amuse ourselves with all manner of follies, and nonsense, and rubbish;" here Aunt Judy chucked the drawing-book to the end of the table, tossed a dictionary after it, and threw another book or two into the air, catching them as they came down.

" - while you, superior, sensible young man that you are, born to be the comfort of your family - "

"Be quiet!" interrupted No. 3, trying to stop her; but she ran round the table and proceeded:-

" - and the enlightener of mankind; can't - no, no, No. 3, I won't be stopt! - can't amuse yourself with anything, because everything is so 'horribly slow, there's nothing to do,' so you want to tie yourself to your foolish sister's apron string."

"It's too bad!" shouted No. 3; and a race round the table began between them, but Aunt Judy dodged far too cleverly to be caught, so it ended in their resting at opposite ends; No. 6 and her French exercises lying between them.

"No. 6, my dear," cried Aunt Judy, in the lull of

exertion, "I proclaim a holiday from folly and rubbish. Put your books away, and put your impertinence away too. Hold your tongue, and don't be Miss Pest; and vanish as soon as you can."

Miss Pert performed two or three putting-away evolutions with the velocity of a sunbeam, and darted off through the door.

"Now, then, we'll be reasonable," observed Aunt Judy; and carrying a chair to the front of the fire she sat down, and motioned to No. 3 to do the same, taking out from her pocket a little bit of embroidery work, which she kept ready for chatting hours.

No. 3 was always willing to listen to Aunt Judy.

He desired nothing better than to get her undivided attention, and pour out his groans in her ear; so he sat down with a very good grace, and proceeded to insist that there never was anything so "slow" as "it was."

Aunt Judy wanted to know what *it* was; the place or the people, (including herself,) or what?

No. 3 could explain it no other way than by declaring that *everything* was slow; there was nothing to do.

Aunt Judy maintained that there was plenty to do.

Whereupon No. 3 said:-

"But nothing *worth* doing."

Whereupon Aunt Judy told No. 3 that he was just like Dr. Faustus. On which, of course, No. 3 wanted to know what Dr. Faustus was like, and Aunt Judy answered, that he was just like *him,* only a great deal older and very learned.

"Only quite different, then," suggested No. 3.

"No," said Aunt Judy, "not *quite* different, for he came one day to the same conclusion that you have done, namely, that there was nothing to do, worth doing in the world."

"*I* don't say the world, I only say here," observed No. 3; "there's plenty to do elsewhere, I dare say."

"So you think, because you have not tried else where," answered Aunt Judy. "But Dr. Faustus, who had tried elsewhere, thought everywhere alike, and declared there was nothing worth doing anywhere, although he had studied law, physic, divinity, and philosophy all through, and knew pretty nearly everything."

"Then you see he did not get much good out of learning," remarked No. 3.

"I do see," was the reply.

"And what became of him?"

"Ah, that's the point," replied Aunt Judy, "and a very remarkable point too. As soon as he got into the state of fancying there was nothing to do, worth doing, in God's world, the evil spirit came to him, and found him something to do in what I may, I am sure, call the devil's world - I mean, wickedness."

"Oh, that's a story written upon Watts's old hymn,"

exclaimed No. 3, contemptuously:-

"'For Satan finds some mischief still,
For idle hands to do.'

Judy! I call that a regular '*sell.*'"

" Not a bit of it," cried Aunt Judy, warmly; "I don't suppose the man who wrote the story ever saw Watts's hymns, or intended to teach anything half as good. It's mamma's moral. She told me she had screwed it out of the story, though she doubted whether it was meant to be there."

"And what's the rest of the story then?" inquired No. 3, whose curiosity was aroused.

"Well! when the old Doctor found the world as it was, so '*slow,*' as you very unmeaningly call it, he took to conjuring and talking with evil spirits by way of amusement; and then they easily persuaded him to be wicked, merely because it gave him something fresh and exciting to do."

"Watts's hymn again! I told you so!" exclaimed No. 3. "But the story's all nonsense from beginning to end. Nobody can conjure, or talk to evil spirits in reality, so the whole thing is impossible; and where you find the moral, I don't know."

No. 3 leant back and yawned as he concluded.

He was rather disappointed that nothing more entertaining had come out of the story of Dr. Faustus.

But Aunt Judy had by no means done.

"Impossible about conjuring and actually *talking* to evil spirits, certainly," said she; "but spiritual influences, both bad and good, come to us all, No. 3, without bodily communion; so for those who are inclined to feel like Dr. Faustus, there is both a moral and a warning in his fate."

"I don't know what about," cried No. 3. "I think he was uncommonly stupid, after all he had learnt, to get into such a mess. Why, you yourself are always trying to make out that the more people labour and learn, the more sure they are to keep out of mischief. Now then, how do you account for the story of your friend Dr. Faustus?"

"Because, like King Solomon, he did not labour and learn in a right spirit, or to a right end," replied Aunt Judy. "Lord Bacon remarks that when, after the Creation, God 'looked upon everything He had made, behold it was *very good;*' whereas when man 'turned him about,' and took a view of the world and his own labours in it, he found that 'all' was 'vanity and vexation of spirit.' Why did he come to such a different conclusion, do you think?"

"I suppose because the world had got bad, before King Solomon's time," suggested No. 3.

"Its inhabitants had," replied Aunt Judy. "They had become subject to sin and misery; but the world was still God's creation, and proofs of the 'very good' which He had pronounced over it were to be found in every direction, and even in fallen man, if Solomon had had the sense, or rather I should say, good feeling to look for them. Ah! No. 3, there was plenty to be learnt and done that would *not* have ended in 'vanity and vexation of spirit' if Solomon had *learnt* in order to trace out the glory of God, instead of establishing his own; and if he had *worked* to create, as far as was in his power, a world of happiness for other people, instead of seeking nothing but his own amusement. If he had worked in the spirit of God, in short."

"But who can? - Nobody," exclaimed No. 3.

"Yes, everybody, who tries, can, to a certain extent," said Aunt Judy. "It only wants the right feeling; some of the good God-like feeling which originated the creation of a beautiful world, and caused the contemplation of it to produce the sublime complacency which is described, 'And God looked upon everything that He had made, and behold it was very good.'"

"It's a sermon, Judy," cried No. 3, half bored, yet half amused at the notion of her preaching; "I'll set up a pulpit for you at once, shall I?"

"No, no, be quiet, No. 3," exclaimed Aunt Judy, "I wish you would try and understand what I say!"

"Well, then," said No. 3, "it appears to me that do what one might now the world has grown bad, it would be impossible to pronounce that '*very good,*' as the result of one's work. There would always be something miserable and unsatisfactory at the end of everything; I mean even if one really was to look into things closely, and work for other people's good, as you say."

"There might be *something* miserable and unsatisfactory, in the result, certainly," answered Aunt Judy; "but that it would *all* be 'vanity and vexation of spirit' I deny. Our blessed Saviour came into the world after

Mrs Alfred Gatty

it had grown bad, remember; and He worked solely for the restoration of the 'very good,' which sin had defaced. It was undoubtedly *miserable* and *unsatisfactory* that He should be rejected by the very creatures He came to help; but when He uttered the words 'It is finished,' the work which He had accomplished, He might well have looked upon and called very good: very very good; even beyond the creation, were that possible."

"There can be no comparison between our Saviour and us," murmured No. 3.

"No," replied his sister; "but only let people work in the same direction, and they will have more 'profit' of their 'labour,' than King Solomon ever owned to, who had, one fears, only learnt, in order to be learned, and worked, to please himself. No man who employs himself in tracing out God's footsteps *in* the world, or in working in God's spirit *for* the world, will ever find such labours end in 'vanity and vexation of spirit!' Solomon, Dr. Faustus, and the grumblers, have only themselves to thank for their disappointment."

"It's very curious," observed No. 3, getting up, and stretching himself over the fire, "I mean about Solomon and Dr. Faustus. But what can one do? What can you or I do? It's absurd to be fancying one can do good to one's fellow-creatures."

"Nevertheless, there is one I want you to do good to, at the present moment," said Aunt Judy - "if it is not actually raining. Don't you remember what despair No. 1 was in this morning, when father sent her off on the pony in such a hurry."

"Ah, that pony! That was just what I wanted myself," interrupted No. 3.

"Exactly, of course," replied Aunt Judy. "But you were not the messenger father wanted, so do not let us go all over that ground again, pray. The fact was, No. 1 had just heard that her pet 'Tawny Rachel' was very ill, and she wanted to go and see her, and give her some good advice, and I am to go instead. Now No. 3, suppose you go instead of me, and save me a wet walk?"

No. 3, of course, began by protesting that it was not possible that he could do any good to an old woman. Old women were not at all in his way. He could only say, how do you do? and come away.

Aunt Judy disputed this: she thought he could offer her some creature comforts, and ask whether she had seen the Doctor, and what he said, as No. 1 particularly wished to know.

What an idea! No, no; he must decline inquiring what the Doctor said; it would be absurd; but he could offer her something to eat.

- And just ask if she had had the Doctor. - Well, just that, and come away. It would not occupy many minutes. But he wished, while Aunt Judy was about it, she had found him something rather *longer* to do!

Aunt Judy promised to see what could be devised on his return, and No. 3 departed. And a very happily chosen errand it was; for it happened in this case, as it so constantly does happen, that what was begun for other people's sake, ended in personal gratification.

Mrs Alfred Gatty

No. 3 went to see "Tawny Rachel," out of good-natured compliance with Aunt Judy's request, but found an interest and amusement in the visit itself, which he had not in the least expected.

Ten, twenty, thirty, minutes elapsed, and he had not returned; and when he did so at last, he burst into the house far more like an avalanche than a young gentleman who could find "nothing to do."

Coming in the back way, he ran into the kitchen, and told the servants to get some hot water ready directly, for he was sure something would be wanted. Then, passing forward, he shouted to know where his mother was, and, having found her, entreated she would order some comfortable, gruelly stuff or other, to be made for the sick old woman, particularly insisting that it should have ale or wine, as well as spice and sugar in it.

He was positive that that was just what she ought to have! She had said how cold she was, and how glad she should be of something to warm her inside; and there was nobody to do anything for her at home. What a shame it was for a poor old creature like that to be left with only two dirty boys to look after her, and they always at play in the street! Her daughter and husband were working out, and she sat moaning over the fire, from pain, without anybody to care!

* * *

Tender-hearted and impulsive, if thoughtless, the spirit of No. 3 had been moved within him at the spectacle of the gaunt old woman in this hour of her lonely suffering.

Poor "Tawny Rachel!" The children had called her so, from the heroine of Mrs. Hannah More's tale, because of those dark gipsy eyes of hers, which had formerly given such a fine expression to her handsome but melancholy face. Melancholy, because care-worn from the long life's struggle for daily bread, for a large indulged family, who scarcely knew, at the day of her death, that she had worn herself out for their sakes.

Poor "Tawny Rachel!" She was one day asked by a well-meaning shopkeeper, of whom she had purchased a few goods, *where she thought she was going to?"*

"Tawny Rachel" turned her sad eyes upon her interrogator, and made answer:-

"Going to? why where do you think I'm going to, but to Heaven? - 'Deed! where do you think I'm going to, but to Heaven?" she repeated to herself slowly, as if to recover breath; and then added, "I should like to know who Heaven is for, if not for such as me, that have slaved all their lives through, for other folk;" and so saying, Tawny Rachel turned round again, and went away.

Poor "Tawny Rachel!" The theology was imperfect enough; but so had been her education and advantages. Yet as surely as her scrupulous, never-failing honesty, and unmurmuring self-denial, must have been inspired by something beyond human teaching; so surely did it prove no difficult task to her spiritual guide, to lead her onwards to those simple verities of the Christian Faith, which, in her case, seemed to solve the riddle of a weary, unsatisfactory life, and, confiding in which, the approach of death really became to her, the advent of the Prince of Peace.

* * *

"But she had quite cheered up," remarked No. 3, "at the notion of something comforting and good," and so - he had "come off at once."

"At once!" - the exclamation came from Aunt Judy, who had entered the room, and was listening to the account. "Why, No. 3, you must have been there an hour at least. And nevertheless I dare say you have forgotten about the Doctor."

"The Doctor!" cried No. 3, laughing, - "It's the Doctor who has kept me all this time. You never heard such fun in your life, - only he's an awful old rascal, I must say!"

Mamma and Aunt Judy gazed at No. 3 in bewilderment. The respectable old village practitioner, who had superintended all the deceases in the place for nearly half a century - to be called "an awful old rascal" at last! What could No. 3 be thinking of?

Certainly not of the respectable village practitioner, as he soon explained, by describing the arrival at Tawny Rachel's cottage of a travelling quack with a long white beard.

"My dear No. 3!" exclaimed mamma.

"Mother, dear, I can't help it!" cried No. 3, and proceeded to relate that while he was sitting with the old woman, listening to the account of her aches and pains, some one looked in at the door, and asked if she wanted anything; but, before she could speak, remarked how ill she seemed, and said he could give her something to do her good. "Judy!" added No. 3, breaking suddenly off; "he looked just like Dr. Faustus, I'm sure!"

"Never mind about that," cried Aunt Judy. "Tell us what Tawny Rachel said."

"Oh, she called out that he *must give* it, if she was to have it, for she had nothing to pay for it with. I had a shilling in my pocket, and was just going to offer it, when I recollected he would most likely do her more harm than good. But the gentleman with the white beard walked in immediately, set his pack down on the table, and said, 'Then, my good woman, I *shall* give it you;' and out he brought a bottle, tasted it before he gave it to her, and promised her that it would cure her if she took it all."

"My dear No. 3!" repeated mamma once more.

"Yes, I know she can't be cured, mother, and I think she knows it too; but still she '*took it very kind,*' as she called it, of him, and asked him if he would like to 'rest him' a bit by the fire, and the gentleman accepted the invitation; and there we all three sat, for really I quite enjoyed seeing him, and he began to warm his hands, remarking that the young gentleman - that was I, you know - looked very well. Oh, Judy, I very nearly said 'Thank you, Dr. Faustus,' but I only laughed and nodded, and really did hold my tongue; and then the two began to talk, and it was as good as any story you ever invented, Aunt Judy. Tawny Rachel was very inquisitive, and asked him:-

"'You've come a long way, sir, I suppose?'

"'Yes, ma'am; I'm a great traveller, and have been so a many years.'

"'It's a wonder you have not settled before now.'

"'I might have settled, ma'am, a many times.'

"'Ah, when folks once begin wandering, they can't settle down. You were, maybe, brought up to it.'

"'I was brought up to something a deal better than that, ma'am.'

"'You was, sir? It's a pity, I'm sure.'

"'My father was physician to Queen Elizabeth, ma'am, a many years.'"

When No. 3 arrived at this point of the dialogue, mamma and Aunt Judy both exclaimed at once, and the former repeated once more the expostulatory "My dear No. 3!" which delighted No. 3, who proceeded to assure them that he had himself interrupted the travelling quack here, by suggesting that it was Queen Charlotte he meant.

"Old Queen Charlotte, you know, Judy, that No. 1 was telling the children about the other day."

But the "gentleman," as No. 3 called him, had turned very red at the doubt thus thrown on his accuracy, and put a rather threatening croak into his voice, as he said:-

"Asking your pardon, young gentleman, I know what I'm saying, and it was Queen Elizabeth, and not

Charlotte nor anybody else!"

No. 3 described that he felt it best, after this, to hold his tongue and say no more, so Tawny Rachel put in her word, and remarked, it was a wonder the queen hadn't made their fortunes; on which the gentleman turned rather red again, and said that the queen did make their fortune, but wouldn't let them keep it, for fear they should be too great and too rich - that was it! This statement required a little explanation, but the gentleman was ready with all particulars. The queen used to pay his father by hundreds of pounds at a time, because that was due to him, but being jealous of his having so much money, she always set some one to take it away from him as he left the place! So that was the reason why these was no fortune put by for him after his father died, and that was the reason why he couldn't very well settle at first, though everybody wished him to stay, and *so* he took to travelling; for his father had left him all his secrets, and he was qualified to practise anywhere, and had cured some thousands of sick folks up and down!

No. 3 declared that he had not made the old man's account of himself a bit more unconnected than it really was, and, on the whole, it sounded very imposing to poor Tawny Rachel, who watched his departure with a sort of respectful awe.

No. 3 added, that not liking to disturb her faith either in the man or the bottle, he had himself helped her to the first dose, and had then begun to talk about the creature comforts before described, the very mention of which seemed to cheer the old lady's heart, and to interest her at least as much as the biography of the travelling quack.

Mrs Alfred Gatty

"So now, mother," concluded he, "order the gruel, and we'll give three cheers for Queen Elizabeth, and Dr. Faustus - eh, Judy? But I do think the poor old thing ought not to take that man's poisonous rubbish; so here's my shilling, and welcome, if you'll give some more, and let us send for a real doctor."

The "nothing-to-do" morning had nearly slipped away, between the conversation with Aunt Judy, and the visit to Tawny Rachel; and when, soon after, a friend called to take No. 3 off on a fossil hunt, and he had to snatch a hasty morsel before his departure, he declared he was like the poor governess in the song, who was sure to

"Find out,
With attention and zeal,
That she'd scarcely have time
To partake of a meal,"

there was so much to do. "But you're a capital fellow, Judy," he added, kissing her, "and you'll tell me a story when I come back;" and off he ran, shutting his ears to Aunt Judy's declaration that she only told stories to the "little ones."

Nor would she, on his return, and during the cozy evening "nothing-to-do" hour, consent to devote herself to his especial amusement only. So, after arguing the point for a time, he very wisely yielded, and declared at last that he would be a "little one" too, and listen to a "little one's" story, if Aunt Judy would tell one.

It was rather late when this was settled, and the little ones had stayed up-stairs to play at a newly-invented game - bazaars - in the nursery; but when No. 3 strode in with the announcement of the story, there was a shout of delight, followed by the old noisy rush downstairs to the dining-room.

It is not a bad thing to be a "little one" now and then in spirit. People would do well to try and be so oftener. Who that has looked upon a picture of himself as a "little one," has not wished that he could be restored to the "little one's" spirit, the "little one's" innocence, the "little one's" hopeful trust? "Of such is the kingdom of Heaven!" And though none of us would like to live our lives over again, lest our errors should be repeated, and so doubled in guilt, all of us, at the sight of what we once were, would fain, very fain, if we could, lie down to sleep, and awake a "little one" again. Never, perhaps, is the sweet mercy of an early death brought so closely home to our apprehension, as when the grown-up, care-worn man looks upon the image of himself as a child.

Happily, however - nay, more than happily, *mercifully* - the grown-up man, if he do but put on the humility, may gain something of the peace of a "little one's" heart!

Aunt Judy had twisted up a roll of muslin for a turban on her head by the time they came down, "for," said she, "this is to be an eastern tale, and I shall not be inspired - that is to say, I shall not get on a bit - unless there is a costume and manners to correspond, so you three little ones squat yourselves down Turkish-fashion on the floor, with your legs tucked under you. There now! that's something like, and I begin to feel myself in the East. Nevertheless, I am rather glad there is no critical Eastern traveller at hand, listening through the key-hole to my blunders.

However, errors excepted, here is the wonderful story of

'THE KING OF THE HILLS AND HIS FOUR SONS.'

"A great many years ago, in a country which cannot be traced upon the maps, but which lies somewhere between the great rivers Indus and Euphrates, lived Schelim, King of the Hills.

"His riches were unlimited, his palaces magnificent, and his dresses and jewels of the most costly description. He never condescended to wear a diamond unless it was inconveniently large for his fingers, and the fiery opals which adorned his turban (like those in the mineral-room at the British Museum) shimmered and blazed in such a surprising manner, that people were obliged to lower their eyes before the light of them.

"Powerful as well as rich, King Schelim could have anything in the world he wished for, but - such is the perversity of human nature - he cared very little for anything except smoking his pipe; of which, to say the truth, he was so fond, that he would have been well contented to have done nothing else all day long. It seemed to him the nearest approach to the sublimest of all ideas of human happiness - the having *nothing to do.*

"He caused his four sons to be brought up in luxurious ease, his wish for them being, that they should remain ignorant of pain and sorrow for as long a period of their lives as was possible. So he built a palace for them, at the summit of one of his beautiful hills, where nothing disagreeable or distressing could ever meet their eyes, and he gave orders to their attendants, that they should never be thwarted in anything.

"Every wish of their hearts, therefore, was gratified from their baby days; but so far from being in consequence the happiest, they were the most discontented children in his dominions.

"From the first year of their birth, King Schelim had never been able to smoke his pipe in peace. There were always messages coming from the royal nursery to the smoking-room, asking for something fresh for the four young princes, who were, owing to some mysterious cause, incapable of enjoying any of their luxurious indulgences for more than a few hours together.

"At first these incessant demands for one thing or another for the children, surprised and annoyed their papa considerably, but by degrees he got used to it, and took the arrival of the messengers as a matter of course.

"The very nurses began it:-

"'May it please your Majesty, the young princes, your Majesty's incomparable sons - may their shadows never be less! - are tired of their jewelled rattles, and have thrown them on the floor. Doubtless they would like India-rubber rings with bells better.'

"'Then get them India-rubber rings with bells,' was all King Schelim said, and turned to his pipe again.

"And so it went on perpetually, until one day it

came to, -

"'May it please your Majesty, the young princes, your Majesty's incomparable sons - may their shadows never be less! - have thrown their hobbyhorses into the river, and want to have live ponies instead.'

"At the first moment the king gave his usual answer, 'Then get them live ponies instead,' from a sort of mechanical habit, but the words were scarcely uttered when he recalled them. This request awoke even his sleepy soul out of its smoke-dream, and inquiring into the ages of his sons, and finding that they were of years to learn as well as to ride, he dismissed their nurses, placed them in the hands of tutors, and procured for them the best masters of every description.

"'For,' said he, 'what saith the proverb? "Kings govern the earth, but wise men govern kings." My sons shall be wise as well as kingly, and then they can govern themselves.'

"And after settling this so cleverly, King Schelim resumed his pipe, in the confident hope, that now, at last, he should smoke it in peace.

"'For,' said he, 'when my sons shall become wise through learning, they will be more moderate in their desires.'

"I do not know whether his Majesty's incomparable sons relished this change from nurses to tutors, but on that particular point they were allowed no choice; so if they bemoaned themselves in their palace on the hill, their father knew nothing of it.

"And to soften the disagreeableness of the restraint which learning imposes, King Schelim gave more strict orders than ever, that, provided the young gentlemen only learnt their lessons well, every whim that came into their heads should be complied with soon as expressed.

"In spite of all his ingenious arrangements, however, the royal father did not enjoy the amount of repose he expected. All was quiet enough during lesson-hours, it is true; but as soon as ever that period had elapsed, the young princes became as restless as ever. Nay - the older they grew, the more they wanted, and the less pleased they became with what was granted.

"From very early days of the tutorship, the old story began:-

"'May it please your Majesty, the young princes, your Majesty's incomparable sons - may their shadows never be less! - are tired of their ponies, and want horses instead.'

"The king was a little disappointed at this, and actually laid down his pipe to talk.

"'Is anything the matter with the ponies?' he asked.

"'May it please your Majesty, no; only that your incomparable sons call them *slow.*'

"'Spirited lads!' thought the king, quite consoled, and gave the answer as usual:-

"'Then get them horses instead.' But when only a few days afterwards he was informed that his incomparable

Mrs Alfred Gatty

sons had wearied of their horses, because they also were 'slow,' and wished to ride on elephants instead, his Majesty began to feel disturbed in mind, and wonder what would come next, and how it was that the teaching of the tutors did not make his sons more moderate in their desires.

"'Nevertheless,' said he, 'what saith the proverb, "Thou a man, and lackest patience?" And again,

"Early ripe, early rotten,
Early wise, soon forgotten."

My sons are but children yet.'

"After which reflection he returned to his pipe as before, and disturbed himself as little as possible, when messenger after messenger arrived, to announce the fresh vagaries of the young princes.

"It is impossible to enumerate all the luxuries, amusements, and delights, they asked for, obtained, and wearied of during several years. But the longer it went on, the more hardened and indifferent their father became.

"'For,' said he, 'what saith the proverb? "The longest lane turns at last." At last my sons will have everything man can wish for, and then they will cease from asking, and I shall smoke my pipe in peace.'

"One day, however, the messenger entered the royal smoking-room in a greater hurry than ever, and was about to commence his usual elaborate peroration respecting the incomparable sons, when his Majesty held up his hand to stop him, and called out:-

"'What is it now?'

"'May it please your Majesty, your Majesty's in - '

"'What is it they *want?*' cried the king, interrupting him.

"'May it please your Majesty, *something to do.*'

"'Something to do?' repeated the perplexed king of the hills; 'something to do, when half the riches of my empire have been expended upon providing them with the means of doing everything in the world that was delightful to the soul of man?

"'Surely, oh son of a dog, thou art laughing at my beard, to come to me with such a message from my sons.'

"'Nevertheless, may it please your Majesty, I have spoken but the truth. Your Majesty's in - '

"'Hush with that nonsense,' interrupted the king.

"'Your Majesty's sons, in fact, then, have sickened and pined for three mortal days, because they have got *nothing to do.*'

"'Now, then, my sons are mad!' exclaimed poor King Schelim, laying down his pipe, and rising from his recumbent position; 'and it is time that I bestir myself.'

"And thereupon he summoned his attendants, and sent for the royal Hakim, that is to say, physician; and the most learned and experienced Dervish, that is to say, religious teacher of the neighbourhood.

"'For,' said he, 'who knows whether this sickness is of the body or the soul?'

"And having explained to them how he had brought up his children, the indulgences with which he had surrounded them, the learning which he had had instilled into them, and the way in which he had preserved them from every annoying sight and sound, he concluded:-

"'What more could I have done for the happiness of my children than I have done, and how is it that their reason has departed from them, so that they are at a loss for something to do? Speak one or other of you and explain.'

"Then the Dervish stepped forward, and opening his mouth, began to make answer.

"'And,' said he, 'oh King of the Hills, in the bringing up of thy sons, surely thou hast forgotten the proverb which saith, "He that would know good manners, let him learn them from him who hath them not." For even so may the wise man say of happiness, "He that would know he is happy, must learn it from him who is not." But again, doth not another proverb say, "Will thy candle burn less brightly for lighting mine?" Wherefore the happiness which a man has, when he has discovered it, he is bound to impart to those that have it not. Have I spoken well?'

"Then King and the Hakim declared he had spoken remarkably well; nevertheless I am by no means sure that King Schelim knew what he meant. Whereupon the Dervish offered to go at once to the four incomparable princes, and cure them of their madness in supposing they had nothing to do, and King Schelim in great delight, and thoroughly glad to be rid of the trouble, told him that he placed his sons entirely in his hands; then taking him aside, he addressed to him a parting word in confidence.

"'Thou knowest, oh wise Dervish, that I have had no education myself, and therefore, as the proverb hath it, "To say *I don't know,* is the comfort of my life," yet what better is a learned man than a fool, if he comes but to this conclusion at last? See thou restore wisdom and something to do to the souls of my sons.'

"Which the Dervish promised to accomplish, accordingly in company with the Hakim, he betook himself to the palace of the four princes, his Majesty's incomparable sons.

"Well, in spite of all they had heard, both the Dervish and Hakim were surprised at what they really found at the palace of the four princes.

"It was as if everything that human ingenuity could devise for the gratification, amusement, and occupation both of body and mind had been here brought together. Horses, elephants, chariots, creatures of every description, for hunting, riding, driving, and all sorts of sport were there, countless in numbers, and perfect in kind. Gardens, pleasure-grounds, woods, flowers, birds, and fountains, to delight the eye and ear; while within the palace were sources of still deeper enjoyment. The songs of the poets and the wisdom of the ancients reposed there upon golden shelves. Musicians held themselves in readiness to pour exquisite melodies upon the air; games, exercises, indoor sports in every variety could be commanded in a moment, and attendants waited in all directions to fulfil their young masters' will.

"The poor old Dervish and Hakim looked at each other in fresh amazement at every step they took, and neither of them could find a proverb to fit so extraordinary a case.

"At last, after a long walk through chambers and anti-chambers without end, hung round with mirrors and ornaments, they reached the apartment of the young princes, where they found the four incomparable creatures lounging on four ottomans, sighing their hearts out, because they had 'nothing to do.'

"As the door opened, the eldest prince glanced languidly round, and inquired if the messenger had returned from their father, and being answered that the Dervish and Hakim, who now stood before him, were messengers from their father, he called out to know if the old gentleman had sent them anything to do!

"'The king, your father's spirit is disturbed with anxiety,' answered the Dervish, 'lest some sudden calamity should have deprived his sons of the use of their limbs or their senses, or lest their attendants should have failed to provide them with everything the earth affords delightful to the soul of man.'

"'The king, our father's spirit is disturbed with smoke,' replied the eldest prince, 'or he never would have sent such an old fellow as you with such an answer as that. What's the use of the use of one's limbs, or one's senses, or all the earth affords delightful to the soul of man, if we're sick of it all? Just go back and tell him we've got everything, and are sick of everything, and can do everything, and don't care to do anything, because everything is so 'slow;' so we will trouble him to find us something fresh to do. There! is that clear enough, old gentleman?'

"'The king, your father,' answered the Dervish, 'has provided against even that emergency; I am come to tell you of something fresh to see and to do.'

"No sooner had the Dervish uttered these words, than the four princes jumped up from the ottoman in the most lively and vigorous manner, and clamoured to know what it was, expressing their hope that it was a 'jolly lark.'

"In answer to which the Dervish, lifting himself up in a commanding manner, stretched out his arm, and exclaimed, in a solemn voice:-

"'Young men, you have exhausted happiness. Nothing new remains in the world for you, but misery and want. Follow me!'

"There was something so unusual about the tone of this address, and it was uttered in so imposing a manner, that the young princes were, as it were, taken by storm, and they followed the Dervish and Hakim, without a word of inquiry or objection.

"And he led them away from the palace on the beautiful hill - away from all the sights and sounds that were collected together there to delight the soul of man with both bodily and intellectual enjoyment - down into the city in the valley, among the close-packed habitations of common men, congregated there to labour, and just exist, and then die.

"And presently the Dervish and the Hakim spoke together, and then the Hakim led the way through a gloomy by-street, till he came to a habitation into which he entered, and the rest followed without a word. And there, stretched upon a pallet, wasted and worn with pain, lay a youth scarcely older than the young princes themselves, the lower part of whose body was wrapped round with bandages, and who was unable to move.

"The Hakim proceeded at once to unloosen the fastenings, and to examine the limbs of the sufferer. They had been crushed by a frightful accident, while working for his daily bread, in the quarries of marble near the palace on the hill.

"'Is there no hope, my father?' he ejaculated in agony as the bruised thighs were exposed to the light, revealing a spectacle from which the princes turned horrified away.

"But the Dervish stood between them and the door, and motioned them back.

"'Is there no hope?' repeated the youth. 'Shall I never again tread the earth in the freedom of health and strength? never again climb the mountain-side to taste the sweet breath of heaven? never again even step across this narrow room, to look forth into the narrow street?'

"Sobs of distress here broke from the speaker; and, covering his face with his hands, he awaited the Hakim's reply. But while the latter bent down to whisper his answer, the Dervish addressed himself to the trembling princes:-

"'Learn here, at last,' said he, 'the value of those limbs, the power of using which you look upon with such thankless indifference. As it is with this youth to-day, so may it be with you to-morrow, if the decree goes forth from on high. Bid me not again return to your father to tell him you are weary of a blessing, the loss of which would overwhelm you with despair.'

"The young princes," continued Aunt Judy, were, as their father had said, but children yet; that is to say, although they were fourteen or fifteen years old, they were childish, in not having reflected or learnt to reason. But they were not hard-hearted at bottom. Their tenderness for others had never been called out during their life of self-indulgence, but the sight of this young man's condition, whom they personally knew as one who had at times been permitted to come up and join in their games, over-powered them with dismay.

"They entreated the Hakim to say if nothing could be done, and when he told them that a nurse, and better food, and the discourse of a wise companion, were all essential for the recovery of the patient, there was not, to say the truth, one among them who was not ready with promises of assistance, and even offers of personal help.

"And now, bidding adieu to this youthful sufferer, whose distress seemed to receive a sudden calm from the sympathy the young princes betrayed, the Hakim led the way to another part of the town, where he entered a house of rather better description, in a small room of which they found a pale, middle-aged man, who was engaged in making a coarse sort of netting for trees. Hearing the noise of the entrance, he looked up, and asked who it was, but with no change of countenance, or apparent recognition of anyone there. But as soon as the Hakim had uttered the words 'It is I,' a gleam of delight stole over the pale face, and the man, rising from his chair, stretched out his arms to the Hakim, entreating him to approach.

"And then the young princes saw that the pale man was blind.

"'Is there any change, oh Cassian?' inquired the Hakim, kindly.

"'None, my father,' answered the blind man, in a subdued tone. 'But shall I murmur at what is appointed? Surely not in vain was the privilege granted me, of transcribing the manuscripts which repose on the golden shelves in the palace of the royal princes. Surely not in vain did I gather, from the treasures of ancient wisdom, and the divine songs of the poets, sources of consolation for the suffering children of men.'

"'And has anyone been of late to read to you?' asked the Hakim.

"But this inquiry the blind man seemed scarcely able to answer. Big tears gathered into the sightless eyes, and folding his hands across his bosom, he murmured out:-

"'None, oh my father. Not to everyone is it permitted to trace the characters of light in which the wise have recorded their wisdom. I alone of my family knew the secret. I alone suffer now. But shall I not submit to this also with a cheerful spirit? It is written, and it behoves me to submit.'

"And, with tears streaming over his cheeks, the blind man took up the netting which he had laid aside, and forced himself to the work.

"'Seest thou!' exclaimed the Dervish, turning to the prince who stood next him, apparently absorbed in contemplating the scene. 'Seest thou how precious are the powers thou hast wearied of in the spring-time of life? How dear are the opportunities thou hast not cared to delight in? Bid me not again return to the king, your father, to tell him his sons can find no pleasure in blessings, the deprivation of which they themselves would feel to be the shutting out of the sun from the soul.'

"Then the young prince to whom the Dervish addressed himself, wept bitterly, and begged to be allowed to visit the blind man from time to time, and read to him out of the manuscripts that reposed on the golden shelves in the palace on the hill; and which, he now learnt for the first time, had been transcribed for his use, and that of his brothers, by the skill of the sufferer before him.

"And when the blind man clasped his hands over his head, and would have prostrated himself on the ground, in gratitude to him who spoke, asking who the charitable pitier of the afflicted could be, the prince embraced him as if he had been his brother, forced him back gently into his seat, and bidding him await him at that hour on the morrow, followed the Hakim from the house.

"And now the Dervish and Hakim spoke together once again, and the place they visited next was of a very different description.

"Enclosed within walls, and limited in extent, because in the outskirts of a populous town, the garden into which they presently entered, was - though but as a drop in comparison with the ocean - no unworthy rival of the gorgeous pleasure-grounds of the palace. There, too, the roses unfolded themselves in their glory to the sun, tiny fountains scattered their cooling spray around, and singing-birds, suspended on over-shadowing trees, of this scene of miniature beauty a venerable was perceived, seated under the shadow of an arbour, in front of a table on which were scattered manuscripts, papers, parchments, and dried plants, and in one corner of which were laid a set of tablets and writing materials.

"Although the door by which they entered had fallen to, with a noise as they passed through, the old man did not seem to be aware of it, nor did he notice their presence until they came so near, that their shadows fell on some of the papers on the table. Then, indeed, he looked suddenly up, and with a smile and gesture of delight, bade them welcome.

"It was not difficult to divine that the old man had lost the sense of hearing, and the Dervish, taking up the tablets from the table, wrote upon them the following words, which he showed to the young princes, before presenting them to him for whom they were intended:-

"'Hast thou not wearied yet, oh brother, of thy narrow garden, and the ever-recurring succession of flowers, and thy study of the secrets of Nature?'

"Whereat the deaf man smiled again, and wrote upon the tablets:-

"'Can anyone weary of tracing out the skilful providence of the Divine Mind? Is it not a world within a world, oh my brother, and inexhaustible in itself?'

"The youngest prince pressed forward to read the answer, and having read it, turned to the Dervish, and said, 'Ask him why the singing-birds are suspended in the garden, whose voices he cannot hear.'

"'Write on the tablet, my son,' said the Dervish; and when he had written it, the old man answered, in the same manner as before:-

"'I would remember my infirmity, my son, lest my soul should be tied to the beauties of the visible world, but now when I see the twittering bills of the feathered songsters, I remember that one sense has departed, and that the others must follow; and I prepare myself for death, trusting that those who have rejoiced in the Divine Mind - however imperfectly - here, may rejoice yet more hereafter, when no sense or power shall be wanting!'

"After this, the venerable old man led them to a secluded corner of the garden, where his young son was instructing one portion of a class of children from the secrets of his father's manuscripts, while another set of youngsters were engaged in cultivating flowers, by regular instruction and rule. Many a bright, cheerful face looked up at the old man and his visitors as they passed, but no one seemed to wish to leave his work, or his lesson, or the kind young tutor who ruled among them.

"'We have wasted our lives, oh my father!' exclaimed

Mrs Alfred Gatty

the young princes, as they passed from this sight. 'Tell us, may we not come back again here, to learn true wisdom from this man and his son?'

"Having obtained the old man's willing consent to his, the Hakim retiring conducted his companions back into the streets; and the young princes, whose eyes were now opened to the instruction they were receiving, came up to the Dervish, and said:-

"'Oh, wise Dervish, we have learnt the lesson you would teach, and we know now that it is but a folly, and a mockery, and a lie, when a man says that he has nothing to do. There is enough to do for all men, if their minds are directed right! Have I not spoken well?'

"'Thou hast spoken well according to thy knowledge,' answered the Dervish, 'but thou hast yet another lesson to learn.'

"The prince was silenced, and the Dervish and Hakim hurried forward to a still different part of the city, where several trades were carried on, and where in one place they came upon an open square, about which a number of gaunt, wild-looking men, were lounging or sitting; unoccupied, listless, and sad.

"'This is wrong, my father, is it not?' inquired one of the princes; but the Dervish, instead of answering him, addressed a man who was standing somewhat apart from the others, and inquired why he was loitering there in idleness, instead of occupying himself in some honest manner?

"The man laughed a bitter mocking laugh, and turning

to his companions, shouted out, 'Hear what the wise man asks! When trade has failed, and no one wants our labour, he asks us why we stand idling here!' Then, facing the Dervish, he continued, 'Do you not know, can you not see, oh teacher of the blind, that we have got *nothing to do*? - *Nothing to do!*' he repeated with a loud cry - '*Nothing to do*! with hearts willing to work, and hands able to work,' - (here he stretched out his bared, muscular arm to the Dervish,) - 'and wife and children calling out for food! Give us *something to do,* thou preacher of virtue and industry,' he concluded, throwing himself on the ground in anguish; 'or, at any rate, cease to mock us with the solemn inquiry of a fool.'

"'Oh, my father, my father,' cried the young princes, pressing forward, 'this is the worst, the very worst of all! All things can be borne, but this dire reality of having *nothing to do*. Let us find them something to do. Let us tear up our gardens, plough up our lawns, and pleasure-grounds, so that we do but find work for these men, and save their children and wives from hunger.'

"'And themselves from crime,' added the Dervish solemnly. Then quitting his companions, he went into the crowd of men, and made known to them in a few hurried words, that, by the order of their young princes, there would, before another day had dawned, be something found to do for them all.

"The cheer of gratitude which followed this announcement, thrilled through the heart of those who had been enabled to offer the boon, and so overpowered them, that, after a liberal distribution of coin to the necessitous labourers, they gladly hurried away.

"'Now my task is ended,' cried the Dervish, as they retraced their steps to the palace on the hill. 'My sons, you have seen the sacred sorrow which may attach to the bitter complaint of having *Nothing to do*. Henceforth seal your lips over the words, for, in all other cases but this, they are, as you yourselves have said, a folly, a mockery, and a lie.'

"It is scarcely necessary to add," continued Aunt Judy, "that the young princes returned to the palace in a very different state of mind from that in which they left it. They had now so many things to do in prospect, so much to plan and inquire about, that when the night closed upon them, they wondered how the day had gone, and grudged the necessary hours of sleep. But on the morrow, just as they were eagerly recommencing their left-off consultations, the Dervish appeared among them, and suggested that their first duty still remained unthought of.

"The incomparable sons were now really surprised, for they had been flattering themselves they were most laudably employed. But the Dervish reminded them, that, although their duty to mankind in general was great, their duty to their father in particular was yet greater, and that it behoved them to set his mind at rest, by assuring him, that henceforth they would not prevent him from smoking his pipe in peace, by restless discontent, and disturbing messages and wants.

"To this the young princes readily agreed, and thoroughly ashamed, on reflection, of the years of harass with which they, in their thoughtless ingratitude, had worried poor King Schelim, they repaired to his presence, and without entering into unnecessary explanations, (which he would not have understood,) assured him that they were perfectly happy, that they had got plenty to do, as well as everything to enjoy, that they were very sorry they had tormented him for so long a period of his life, but that they begged to be forgiven, and would never do so again!

"King Schelim was uncommonly pleased with what they said, although he had to lay down his pipe for a few minutes to receive their salutations, and give his in return; after which they returned to their palace on the hill, and led thenceforward useful, intelligent, and therefore happy lives, reforming grievances, consoling sorrows, and taking particular care that everybody had the opportunity of having *something to do.*

"And as they never again disturbed their father King Schelim, with foolish messages, he smoked his pipe in peace to the end of his days."

"Nice old Schelim!" observed No. 8, when Aunt Judy's pause showed that the story was done. A conclusion which made the other little ones laugh; but now Aunt Judy spoke again.

"You like the story, all of you?"

Could there be a doubt about it? No! "Schelim, King of the Hills, and his four sons," was one of Aunt Judy's very, very, very, best inventions. But they had the happy knack of always thinking so of the last they heard.

"And yet there is a flaw in it," said Aunt Judy.

"Aunt Judy!" exclaimed several voices at once, in a tone of expostulation.

"Yes; I mean in the moral:" pursued she, "there is no Christianity in the teaching, and therefore it is not perfect, although it is all very good as far as it goes."

"But they were eastern people, and I suppose Mahometans or Brahmins," suggested No. 4.

"Exactly; and, therefore, I could not give them Christian principles; and, therefore, although I have made my four princes turn out very well, and do what was right, for the rest of their lives (as I had a right to do); yet it is only proper I should explain, that I do not believe any people can be *depended upon* for doing right, except when they live upon Christian principles, and are helped by the grace of God, to fulfil His will, as revealed to us by His Son Jesus Christ.

"Certainly it is always more *reasonable* to do right than wrong, even when the wrong may seem most pleasant at the moment; because, as all people of sense know, doing right is most for their own happiness, as well as for everybody else's, even in this world.

"But although the knowledge of this may influence us when we are in a sober enough state of mind to think about it calmly, the inducement is not a sufficiently strong one to be relied upon as a safe-guard, when storms of passion and strong temptations come upon us. In such cases it very often goes for nothing, and then it is a perfect chance which way a person acts.

"Even in the matter of doing good to others, we need the Christian principle as our motive, or we may be often tempted to give it up, or even to be as cruel at some moments, as we are kind at others. It is very pleasant, no doubt, to do good, and be charitable, when the feeling comes into the heart, but the mere pleasure is apt to cease, if we find people thankless or stupid, and that our labours seem to have been in vain. And what a temptation there is, then, to turn away in disgust, unless we are acting upon Christ's commands, and can bear in mind, that even when the pleasure ends, the duty remains.

"And now," said Aunt Judy in conclusion, "a kiss for the story-teller all round, if you please. She has had an invitation, and is going from home to-morrow."

"Oh, Aunt Judy!" ejaculated the little ones, in not the most cheerful of tones.

"Well," cried Aunt Judy, looking at them and laughing, "you don't mean to say that you will not find *plenty to do,* and *plenty to enjoy* while I am away? Come, I mean to write to you all by turns, and I shall inquire in my letters whether you have remembered, *to your edification,* the story of Schelim, King of the Hills, and his four sons."

Footnotes:

{1} "Weide," pasture, grass.

www.ingramcontent.com/pod-product-compliance
Lightning Source LLC
Chambersburg PA
CBHW031351170626
46807CB00002B/920